I0702883

A.W. BALDWIN
MOONSHINE MESA

ISBN	979-8-9884895-0-4 Hardbound
ISBN	979-8-9884895-1-1 Paperback
ISBN	979-8-9884895-2-8 ebook

Cover art by Daniel Thiede.
Map art by Nate Baldwin

For all who manage to teach us something, despite ourselves

and

*For all the Liv-Moor Drive Irregulars – you know
who you are!*

Award-Winning Novels by A. W. Baldwin

MOONSHINE MESA

"…a sleuth murder mystery, crime-drama thriller, and action novel all rolled into one page-turner"

"witty dialogue and humor…[with] vibrant characters whose personalities leap off the pages"

"I especially loved it when Deputy Dawson briefly joined the duo of Parker and Relic, creating a fascinating dynamic between the three. If you enjoy crime capers, dry humor, and quirky characters, you won't go wrong with Moonshine Mesa."

"an action and suspense story that paces itself at a near sprint"

— *Readers' Favorite Five Star Reviews*

"a captivating narrative filled with suspense, mystery, and unexpected twists."

"a gripping tale of mystery, intrigue, and environmental peril."

— *Literary Titan 5 Star Review*

THE ANTIDOTE

Can a botany student, a couple of old-timers, and genetically modified seeds provide the antidote for climate change? The cross-hairs on those million-dollar seeds are on them, too…

"This harrowing techno-thriller is an impressive achievement – timely, and rich with research, intrigue, and a main character you will be rooting for from the beginning all the way to the exhilarating climax. Highly recommended!"

> *– #1 Amazon Best-selling author Landon Beach (The Wreck, Narrator).*

"The chemistry between Harry and Keaton is electrifying." "…there is never a dull moment…The Antidote [is] a gripping novel."

> *– Readers' Favorite Five Star Reviews*

BROKEN INN

The mob, undercover agents, and secret payloads make Broken Inn a dangerous place for a fresh reporter, a newspaper photographer, and a moonshining hermit.

"The desert bakes while the danger scorches in another outstanding mystery from A.W. Baldwin."
> *– #1 New York Times Bestselling Author Dirk Cussler.*

Winner of awards from the Grand Master Adventure Writer's Competition, New York City Big Book Awards, Independent Press Awards, Global Book Awards, and Books Shelf Writing Awards.

WINGS OVER GHOST CREEK

Can a moonshining hermit, a reluctant pilot, and a misfit student uncover the truth and escape an archeology field class that hides assassins and dealers in black-market treasure?

Baldwin has a "gift for capturing the reader's attention at the beginning and keeping them spellbound."
— *Onlinebookclub.org review*

Winner of awards from the Grand Master Adventure Writer's Competition and Global Book Awards; Reader's Favorite Five Star Review.

RAPTOR CANYON

Armed with a full box of toothpicks (and a little dynamite), can a moonshining hermit, a big-city lawyer, and a student with secret ties to the site monkey-wrench a corrupt land deal and recast the fate of Raptor Canyon?

"A gem of a read…"
> *– #1 New York Times best-selling author*
> *Dirk Cussler*

"[You'll be] holding your heart and your breath at the same time…"
> *– Peter Greene, award winning author of The*
> *Adventures of Jonathan Moore series*

"A hoot of an adventure novel…"
> *– - Reader's Favorite.*

Grand Master Adventure Writer's Finalist Award and Screencraft Cinematic Book Contest Semi-finalist; Reader's Favorite Five Star Review.

DIAMONDS OF DEVIL'S TAIL

When diamonds appear in a remote canyon stream, whitewater rafters and artifact thieves set off in a deadly race to the source.

"Relic is a unique and intriguing character…passionately interested in preserving the ancient archeological sites and conserving the land and water…[We] enthusiastically recommend it to readers who enjoy thrillers, action-packed adventure, and crime novels."
— *Onlinebookclub.org four out of four Star Review.*

"Another rollicking Relic ride from A.W. Baldwin…a bunch of double-crossing, dirt dealing, diamond thieves run into Relic's trademark wit and ingenuity. Enjoy!"
— *Jacob P. Avila, Cave Diver.*

"…an adeptly written thriller…the excitement and tension are superb…the
entire plot [is] compelling"
— *Readers' Favorite Five Star Review.*

DESERT GUARDIAN

A moonshining hermit; a campus bookworm; a midnight murder. Can an unlikely duo and a whitewater crew save themselves and an ancient Aztec battlefield from deadly looters?

Desert Guardian is an "engaging action… mystery" with "tough, credible characters."
> – *Readers' Favorite Five Star Review.*

Buy now from a bookstore near you or amazon.com
For more about these award-winning books go to:
AWBALDWIN.COM

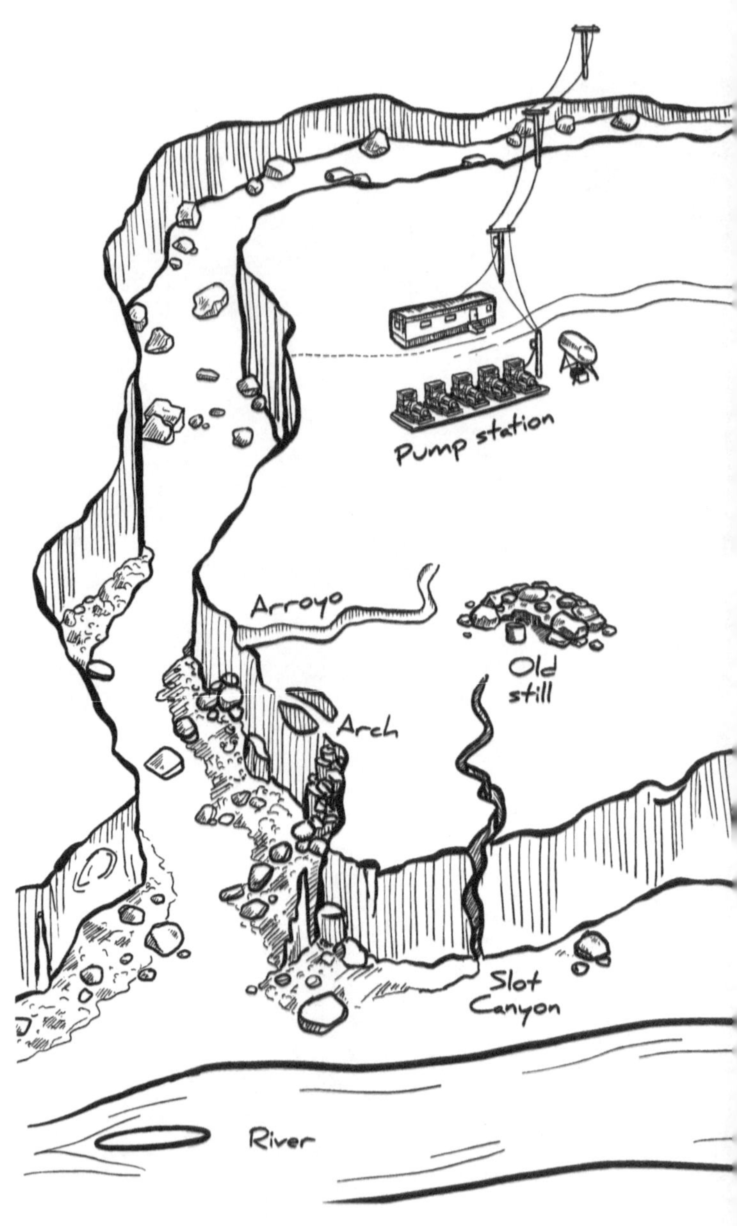

Pump station
Arroyo
Old still
Arch
Slot Canyon
River

N
W
S
E
Ruins
River

CHAPTER 1

"Time to dot my tees…and cross my eyes."

Relic touched his finger close to the body of the dead honeybee. Twelve or more lay along a shallow crack in the rock like a string of Christmas lights, unplugged.

He'd rappelled down a slickrock canyon northwest of a set of ancient pueblo ruins known as Cedar Flute, named after a handsome wooden flute found in one of the larger homes. These stone dwellings lay near the center of the Colorado Plateau, a vast area formed three hundred million years ago by the rise and retreat of shallow, inland seas; a time when fish first learned how to crawl onto land.

He'd found a similar line of bees above the canyon on Moonshine Mesa. They seemed to be leading toward the ruins. Or maybe away from them.

He adjusted the pack on his shoulders and made his way across open ground to the base of the sandstone cliffs—gargantuan, two-hundred-million-year-old sand dunes. He searched the ground for more bees, or other signs of interest, but found none. He hiked another mile to a corner of the high bluffs, where the land opened to his left, a place just upriver from the ruins.

He tucked his raven-colored hair into a ponytail and ran a calloused finger through his thin goatee. A descendant of disparate clans of Hopi and Scottish, Relic was a recluse of these canyons, moonshining some of the time, wandering all of the time, exploring the allure of the Green and Colorado Rivers, their jagged canyons, chiseled cliffs, dizzying spires. He scratched between his eyes.

What the hell had killed those honeybees?

Human voices blended into a stream of whispers, floating on the canyon breeze. Cedar Flute was the subject of an archaeological dig and partial stabilization. Just last week, he'd seen a crew of students and professors staking areas for sample excavations. Careful measurements and re-stacking of stone walls had been undertaken, including the addition of fresh adobe mud used like concrete to secure each of the sandstone blocks.

A black feather fluttered past, twirling on a gust of wind.

He stepped farther around the high corner, walking toward the ruins, following the muted sounds of activity. He reached a tall boulder at the northern end of the old pueblo complex and peered around it.

A dead crow lay forty feet from him.

Beyond that, a lone dwelling stood apart from the others, one he'd dubbed the "mother-in-law suite." The casita was remarkably well preserved, its ruddy stone walls still intact, the rectangular entrance black as outer space. To his right spread a flood plain dotted with grasses and sage and prickly pear—an area farmed by the Pueblo people who lived here ten centuries ago.

He walked to the crow and examined it. Though crows are scavengers, they are intelligent and highly social animals. They will not eat one of their own. The body was still fresh, undisturbed by coyotes or red-tailed hawks or anything else. Had it died mid-flight? What could have killed it without leaving any wounds or marks on it?

Odd.

He rounded the boulder and the sounds of scuffling boots and scraping trowels grew much louder. He moved closer to the mother-in-law suite, stepping into a depression in the ground near a crack in the cliffs.

There in the dust lay a man with a knapsack, silent and still as the old crow.

He hurried to the man's side and felt for a pulse.

The man lay on his stomach, his face sideways in the dirt, a single blue eye over-dilated, staring into a distant void.

No pulse.

What had happened here?

"Professor!"

The voice jolted him upright and he stared at a skinny student with a shovel in one hand, a notebook in the other. The young man stopped short, dropping the book to the ground, eyes wide, mouth open.

Relic held up the palm of his hand and started to speak.

"Hey," the student yelled over Relic's words and raised his shovel in the air. "Get away from him!"

Relic took a step back. "He's dead…"

"Help! Help!" the young man shouted behind him then spun and pulled the shovel to his shoulder, a baseball player ready to swing. Then he charged.

Relic stepped aside as the shovel swung past his head.

Three more students trotted into view.

Enough of this.

The young man recovered from his reckless swing and quickly tried again, his arms shifting with nervous energy. Relic leaned away just in time and then, as the man twisted past, Relic tripped him with his foot. The student spun downward, falling over the dead man, landing hard into the dirt.

Relic scooted behind the tall boulder and began an easy lope away from the commotion.

He hadn't started this trouble, whatever it was.

CHAPTER 2

Parker crossed North Avenue to the Summit Professional Building, a four-story office suite in Grand Junction framed with half-pillars shaped like columns of the Roman Pantheon, out of place and self-important. Furnished with plush conference rooms and a modern auditorium for film or in-person presentations, the Summit housed a large accounting firm, several real estate agents, and a tax advice service. The primary tenant was Redding, Welsh, Belknap, and Story. The firm had twenty lawyers representing corporate interests all over the West and a civil and criminal defense section with clients as far away as Denver and even Phoenix. Parker worked for Betty Coulter, property manager for Sapphire Solutions, a company wholly owned by the firm with multiple business holdings in Colorado and Utah. She managed the Summit Building and the other properties.

He balanced a cardboard tray with four hot lattés

in his left hand and opened the glass doors.

Parker had wanted dual degrees in political science and business administration but dropped out two years ago when his little sister Mia died at a high school graduation party. She'd overdosed on fentanyl in a Denver suburb, her life cut short in a moment of bad judgment. That was all it took—one mere moment, one incautious choice. Their father had turned morose, their mother a nervous wreck. He knew the stages of grief, of course, and just when he thought he'd reached the end, just when he thought he'd come to accept what had happened, he seemed to circle back to that acidic second stage: anger. But he'd been doing better lately. The abrupt end to college had left him a little untethered, but he'd been searching for the next big challenge, the next steps in his life, and that effort itself had been therapeutic. He wondered whether he'd found the right ambition yet. He'd been thinking about law school or related work, which was part of what brought him to Redding, Welsh, Belknap, and Story.

He'd begun working for Betty Coulter two weeks ago, but he'd also been trying to develop a friendship with Charles Story, one of the law partners and lead attorney in the criminal law division, and his cute administrative assistant, Cindy. Two of the lattés were for them.

The third latté was for Dominic, who also worked for Betty Coulter. A retired petroleum worker with granddaughters nearby, Dom could rewire a sound system or diagnose an oil pump mishap as easily as he could change a light bulb.

Parker walked across the terrazzo floor and through a door next to the auditorium marked "maintenance." The room opened to a large storage area with metal shelves full of lightbulbs, electrical switches, computer cables, and boxes of stuff that only Dom would keep. A lone desk sat in the far-left corner near another door, swimsuit calendar posted above a swivel chair. Parker put the tray of coffee between the phone and a painted hula bobble-doll that twisted at the waist. He went through the door into the auditorium. Dom was moving slowly down an iron ladder bolted to the wall behind a theater-style curtain. The ladder led to a labyrinth of walkways atop the ceiling, access to the electrical fixtures that lit the large room.

"Where's a young kid when I need 'mi?" Dom brushed the dust from his jeans. Five-foot-eight with a crew cut that added another half inch, Dom rounded his shoulders and stretched his back, the muscle memory of an old weightlifter.

"I'm twenty-four years old."

"Just outta diapers." Dom's pale eyes flashed a hint of mischief.

"Got you a latté," Parker stepped closer. "Changing lightbulbs again?" He pointed at the tile hatchway above them. "That's dangerous work, Dom. You fall through," he motioned with his hands, "and you'll be the star of the show down here."

Parker had been up there once, sliding across narrow planks to reach the fixtures, no room to sit or stand, nothing but molded pieces of foam between the crawlway and the rows of theater seats thirty to fifty feet below. Just the thought of it aggravated his anxiety about heights.

"Humph." Dom pulled red velvet curtains over the built-in ladder.

"It's getting cold." Parker pointed toward the lattés and led the way back into the office. Once there, he placed them on Dom's desk.

"Four of 'em? Who else you buttering up this morning?" Dom caught up to him and lifted a coffee from the tray.

"Mr. Story…"

Dom stared at Parker from under his brow.

"Hey, I'm interested in his cases…"

"Sure, sure. And who else?"

"Well…" Parker glanced at his feet.

"Not Cindy?" Dom straightened his back.

"What?"

"Parker…"

"…what?"

"You don't see it?"

Parker took the tray from the desk. "I see chemistry between us." His nose turned up in mock formality.

"I see drama."

Parker's neck tensed. He liked Dom, but who was he to tell Parker who he could be interested in? "We'll see."

"You're just chasing a nice pair of legs."

Parker leaned to his left to better see the calendar girl on the wall behind Dom's desk, hips and legs airbrushed to perfection. "Hmmm."

Dom ignored Parker's subtle rebuttal and asked: "How can you be sweet on a girl you don't even know?"

It happens these days. He'd had an on-again, off-again girlfriend until last fall, a woman with a great smile who he'd been trying mightily to forget. She'd moved to Oregon for a post-graduate degree, or so she'd said. He didn't miss the downs in their relationship, but when things were good, well, he sure missed waking up with her in the morning. He'd been conditioning himself not to think of her name anymore, but progress on that had been slow. He was hoping Cindy could help.

And Cindy could also get him closer to Charles Story, the famous defense lawyer, who could explain the ins and outs of law school. Parker was moving forward, he told himself; a man with a plan.

CHAPTER 3

Relic hiked into a narrow opening in the rugged cliffs, the small side canyon he'd descended to reach the Cedar Flute ruins. Thirty feet at the opening, the sandstone walls gradually closed to twenty, fifteen, then ten feet across, massive sides blocking the scorching sun. He walked around errant rocks, fallen from the heights above, retracing his own footprints deeper into the shadows.

When he reached a sharp rock wedged in a crack, he began to climb loose scree and boulders that rose quickly from the canyon floor. Fifty feet higher, the rock fall petered out at the base of a chiseled spire a hundred feet above him.

On his way down, he'd left his harness and climbing rope in place.

He stepped into the nylon straps and roped in for the climb. He reached for a hand-hold above his head, lifted himself upward, and found an edge for his boot.

Climbing shoes would be much easier to use, but the ascent here was not very technical. He preferred to use his helmet, too, but he'd left both of them at a base camp. There was only so much gear he could haul around, and he hadn't expected to do much climbing on this trip.

Tightening the rope as he went, Relic continued up the rugged face, hand-hold to hand-hold, until he reached a three-foot-wide ledge where he'd tied off his rope to a small juniper tree. Balanced there, he undid the rope, wound it into loops, and stored it on the outside of his pack. From there, he scrambled another hundred feet to the top of the plateau, unbuckled his harness, and sat for a rest.

A fresh breeze carried the scent of sage from across the mesa. He hiked a mile across the flats to a rocky outcrop and found the small shelter he was looking for. Beneath a cap of sandstone fifteen feet high lay the remnants of an old moonshine still, one of three on the mesa that gave the place its name. A faint two-track ran to the east, grown over with grass and brush. A tiny spring on this spot had dried up over the last decade. The still itself had been out of commission since the 1930s, when the nation finally realized that people were going to drink alcohol whether it was illegal or not.

When liquor was outlawed, only outlaws had liquor.

Relic's Scottish grandfather, one of those very hooligans, had taught Relic the tricks of the trade. Relic's largest still needed parts from time to time, and he hoped to find something useful in the remains here. Waste not, want not.

He used simple, copper stills in two locations hidden in the outback. Crushed corn, spring water, sugar, and a dash of yeast created a fermented mash. The column-shaped still distilled the mash, heating it until the alcohol steamed into a spiral of metal tubing, where it cooled and dripped into a separate container.

Relic searched the ground, digging an inch or two in spots, breaking up the sandy soil. A sheet of old copper lay against the back of the shelter, too eaten up with age to be of any use now. But a few feet away, he dug up a pair of elbow joints in fair condition. They might make good replacement parts, so he blew the dirt out of them and tucked them in a side pocket of his pack.

He sat at the edge of the shelter and rubbed his chin. He had no clue what had killed the man he'd found near the ruins, but he hadn't seen any sign of a fight or a head wound or blood. It was especially odd that the dead bees and crow seemed to lead him to the man's body. The other people at the ruins, the students there, seemed to be alright.

Had the dead man been sick? Could it have been a heart attack?

He decided to see if he could find those bees again and follow them in the other direction this time. To the east, across the plateau.

A string of death leading to the ruins, or away from them, could not be a coincidence.

CHAPTER 4

Parker turned away from Dom. "Gotta get these coffees upstairs before they get cold. Then I'll be back down to find Betty and see what she's got us doing today." Parker left the office, closing the door behind him. He moved quickly across the polished floor and into an elevator. After a quick ride, the doors opened to a broad, oak counter with the words Redding, Welsh, Belknap, & Story in raised gold letters.

He walked through a glass doorway to a wide hall with offices on the left and a reception area farther down and toward the corner of the building. He passed a conference room and snuck a peek through the door. Ryan, an attorney, and Melinda, a paralegal with her brunette hair tied in a bun, sat staring at papers spread across the tabletop. He'd met them once but hadn't had much opportunity to get to know them. Melinda glanced at him just as he passed by, a quick smile on her lips that might have been meant for him, but he was past the door before he could respond in kind.

Cindy, Charles Story's administrative assistant, sat behind her desk, blonde hair touching her shoulders, gaze locked onto her computer screen. He took a breath and moved toward Story's office.

Cindy glanced up at him, a question in her hazel eyes.

"Got lattés for me and Dom, and… they had a coupon…" He fibbed about the coupon, but his nerves were fluttering. "So, I got a couple for you and Mr. Story."

"Thanks, uh…" she stopped typing.

"Parker." His cheeks warmed.

"Right, I know. I'll get it to Mr. Story." She smiled quickly at him and focused again on the computer screen.

"Sure. Yeah. Thanks." He stayed where he stood.

"Yes?" She looked up at him again, a polite but professional question.

"The thing is, I need to talk to Mr. Story for just a quick moment. Maybe I could bring him the latté?"

"I don't know…"

Charles Story suddenly opened his office door, leaning into the reception room. "Aren't you Mister Parker Barnes?"

He wasn't used to being called a mister. "Yes, sir,"

Parker moved toward the lawyer. "I wanted to meet you for a minute, and I brought coffee…"

"Smart man," Charles stepped forward and pulled a latté from the tray. "I have a minute. Step inside." He moved from the open doorway and waved at Parker to enter. "I'm expecting Mr. Smith in about twenty," he said to Cindy. "Let me know as soon as he arrives."

"Of course," her head bobbed.

Parker stepped inside Charles's office and moved toward his desk. Plate glass windows framed a view of red rock cliffs and the rugged plateau above them that formed a national monument. The Colorado River snaked between the office and the cliffs, light brushing against the water, glaring in the distance.

"Sit, Mr. Barnes." Close-cropped gray hair covered Charles's head, merging seamlessly into a bearded jaw and mustache. A dark blue suit hung from his shoulders in a perfect fit, silver pin-striping woven through silken cloth, his shoes polished to a high-end gloss. He and his partners had built the firm into a powerhouse in the region, a professional and economic success, and he certainly dressed the part.

Charles pulled wire glasses from his face and set them on his desk, then lowered himself into a chair. Blue eyes examined Parker like a surgeon preparing to operate, but then a smile rose on his lips. "You're the new assistant property manager, right? Helping Betty Coulter?"

Parker nodded.

"Tell me about yourself."

He told Charles he was interested in attending law school and that he appreciated the opportunity to work for the firm, hoping he didn't sound like an ass-kisser and fearing that he did. Parker couldn't help but notice the vintage silver Jaguar that Charles drove to the office each day, an antique that showcased the man's status in the city. That and thousand-dollar suits and his name in gold on a classy office building near the center of town. Defending corporate enterprises could be big business.

"Where did you go to school?" Parker asked.

"Oh, don't get me started on law school," Charles leaned back in his chair and gazed at the ceiling. "Too many memories," he smiled.

"I was really impressed with Boxer v Oliver," Parker said. He figured one way to connect was to research some of the cases handled by the law partner.

Charles's brow rose higher on his forehead.

"I know it was your case, and it clarified the supreme court standard for Daubert motions—requests to a court to restrict potential evidence a jury can see at trial."

"You're remarkably well informed, Mr. Barnes."

"I'm just hoping some of your expertise will rub off on me," Parker said.

"You're interested in trial work, I take it."

"Yes."

"Criminal law is the way to get to trial quickly, and get lots of trial experience," Charles leaned forward, arms on the desk.

"I'd love just five minutes of your advice about practicing law."

"Sure. That'll be $1,500." He leaned back again, another smile on his face.

Parker smiled, too, but he knew it was not so far from reality to be a joke. The firm had handled some of the most challenging defenses against tax evasion and personal injury claims in the state, and the partners charged top dollar.

"Mr. Story?" Cindy leaned her head past the doorway, lemon hair angled across her neck. "Mr. Smith is on his way down the hallway." She moved back to her desk, partly visible through the glass wall.

"A long-time client," Charles whispered to Parker and rose from his chair. "They tried to get him on conspiracy, money laundering. We kicked their ass every time," Charles smiled as he spoke, words slipping through his lips like a ventriloquist.

Parker stood, too, making his way toward the door but staying to the side. Could this be the defendant in the notorious State v Smith trial from two years ago? He'd seen a news story at the time but didn't realize that Charles had represented him.

Cindy smiled a row of snowy white teeth and waved Smith into the office.

The man was probably six foot six, a full head taller than Parker, his face ruddy and stern, an old scar along the edge of his right jaw. Coal colored hair clung to a slightly misshapen skull. His deep blue suit blocked the light from the outer office, darkening the doorway.

Indeed, this was the infamous fentanyl dealer saved from a life in prison. By Parker's new over-boss, Charles Story.

Parker's throat closed.

Cheap, easy to transport, and powerfully addictive, Parker knew that fentanyl had become the drug of choice for dealers and users alike and the single leading cause of accidental deaths in America. The illicit drug trade was booming with it. One hundred times stronger than morphine, its victims ran the gamut from the homeless to middle-class moms to Hollywood stars. To high school seniors, like his sister.

The trial had been a circus played out in the media. The prosecutor had overcharged and had mis-handled some of the forensics. His evidence was thin except for one key witness who later recanted his story. The jury did not convict. Several local teens had died of overdoses from fentanyl undoubtedly supplied by Smith. The results of these criminal cases had devastated the victim's families.

Parker felt an involuntary shiver.

One year later, a racketeering charge against Smith was tossed out of court before it reached a trial; the evidence based on an illegal search of one of the distributor's associates. More of Charles's work, he assumed.

"Please come in, Mr. Smith," Charles said. "I've got a fresh latté here for you." The coffee Parker had brought for Charles was going to the drug dealer.

"This is our new assistant property manager, Parker Barnes," Charles motioned toward him.

Smith flashed a smile at Parker like he'd patted a youngster on the head, quick and condescending. The tooth in front of his canine was silver.

Parker waved quickly at Charles and slid out of the office, closing the door behind him.

CHAPTER 5

Betty pulled the ends of her hair into her mouth, a teenage habit that had lasted decades. She glanced at her Manager of the Year award, hanging on the wall opposite her desk. Window blinds reflected against her computer screen, slashing white lines across a chart full of readings—numbers showing pounds per square inch, ambient temperatures, volumes and pressures on each of a dozen pumps at the old oil field.

She frowned.

Pressure readings had dropped dramatically. Temperatures were good and volumes just as they'd predicted, but the psi, the pounds per square inch, were way off.

She pulled the hair from her mouth and tucked it behind her ear. Fifty-five years old, Betty managed property for Sapphire Solutions, a company wholly owned by the law firm. The company had acquired a nearly depleted oil field in Utah twelve years ago and owned three office buildings and a printing center in Grand Junction, Colorado. She'd had no children and divorced nearly twenty-five years ago. Ever since, she'd devoted her life to her work and to the one man in her life, her boss and managing partner of the law firm: Charles Story.

She slid the cursor across the screen a few times, but of course none of the numbers on the spreadsheet changed.

What did the low readings mean?

She had to take this to Charles.

Betty printed the screen to her in-office printer, stood, and straightened her blouse. She checked herself in an old compact-style mirror, turning her face from side to side, fluffing her shoulder-length hair and checking the roots for signs of gray. Though her figure had thickened over the years, she could still turn a few heads and she smiled at the thought. She folded the page in half and walked to the foyer on the first floor.

"Morning," she nodded at Rodney, long-time security guard for the building. His station sat across from the elevators.

"Morning, Miss Coulter," he smiled.

She enjoyed being referred to as "miss," and of course Rodney, that unabashed flirt, knew it. She rode the elevator to the fourth floor and walked to Cindy's desk, Charles's new administrative assistant.

"Is Charles in today?"

Cindy had been only six weeks on the job, a twenty-something business graduate with flowing blond hair and a slender figure. Betty tried not to hate her for it.

"Yes, his last client just left," Cindy pointed to Charles's door.

"I'll just be a moment," Betty moved past the desk before Cindy could stop her. She'd made it a point to show Cindy that she could walk in on Charles anytime he was alone in his office—she did not need Charles's permission and certainly not Cindy's.

Charles Story looked up from this computer as Betty closed the door behind her. At sixty-six, Charles was also a divorcee. He was not only a founding partner of the law firm but also a driving force in the firm's investments in regional properties. With wire-rim glasses and a handsome gray beard, she knew that he was looking forward to retirement this year. He'd already negotiated a deal to sell his shares of the firm, but contrary to what most people thought, the shares were no ticket to riches. Although the firm was busy and successful, the value of a lawyer's name after he or she left a firm was less than inspiring. In fact, he expected the valuation next year to remain in the low six-digit range; for him, not even enough to get through one full year of retirement.

Betty had secretly harbored feelings for Charles for years. Eleven months ago, he'd reached out to her, and they'd begun dating clandestinely. Keeping their relationship quiet at the office tested her resolve nearly to the breaking point, but every weekday at eight in the morning she drank a double latté and walled off her feelings.

On weekends, they'd found themselves working on the old oil field project, and when they began fantasizing about retiring together on a sunny beach, her heart had nearly exploded.

When Betty realized the opportunity the energy project presented, she'd worked even harder to bring it to fruition. Oil revenue was declining but funds for green energy were on the rise, the financing loose and plentiful.

"Good morning. You look a little…concerned," Charles slid to the center of his desk and leaned forward.

Her lips tightened and she nodded at the printout in her hand. "Weird numbers." She handed him the papers.

He removed his glasses and examined the documents.

"I'm not sure what's causing this…" She sat in the chair across from his desk.

"Me neither," he mumbled.

"Our next report is due in a week."

"Right. Let's hope these are an anomaly. But we'd better find out quickly."

She released a sigh and put her hands on the edge of the desk.

"But don't worry too much about this. We'll figure it out." He gave her a quick smile.

"There's a lot riding on it." She squeezed her fingers together, feeling some chagrin at having reminded him. He knew full well that their retirement accounts, their seaside villa, their romantic future together, depended on the success of this project. She could practically taste the ocean air on her tongue.

"Any ideas on how to fix it?" He leaned toward her.

"I'll figure out something." She nodded.

"I've always found Mr. Smith to be a resourceful fellow." Charles's pale eyes narrowed. "If it becomes something serious."

Smith—if that was his birth name—had ties with fentanyl importers in that region of the country where four states came together: Colorado, Utah, Arizona, and New Mexico. Allegedly, he'd become an important lieutenant in the illegal trade, a problem-solver for the kingpins. Smith came to Charles on a regular basis for confidential advice, careful to avoid discussions about any on-going criminal activity that would not be subject to the attorney-client privilege. He also brought a steady stream of referrals to the firm, often paying top dollar. Smith felt like he owed Charles a duty of loyalty, a feeling Charles encouraged.

"The numbers on these gauges did take a pretty big drop." She touched the pages in his hand.

"We get these readings over the internet, right?" he asked.

"Yes, and they go only to me. I include the numbers in our reports to the grantor."

"Let's hope it's just the gauges. I mean, that would explain it and we can replace them easily enough."

"What if it's not?"

He stared into her eyes for a moment. "Let's ask Dom to go out there. An on-site inspection. Have him check the gauges and the pumps himself and report back to you. In-house, so to speak."

"That way..." she nodded slowly, "if the problem is bigger than just the gauges, we can figure out our next step."

"Exactly." He tapped the papers on his desktop, straightening them into a neat stack.

"I'll send Dom out there right away. And maybe the new guy."

"New guy?"

"Parker."

"Oh, yes, of course. Met him earlier today. He's job mentoring under Dom, right?"

"Right."

"Then send them both. Tell them you want a phone call but there's no need for a memo or anything written. Until we know more."

"And if it's the gauges?"

"He'll do a memo to you, and we'll replace the gauges and put it all in a report to the funding source."

"And if it's not the gauges?"

He cast her a knowing look.

Right, she thought. Talk to Mr. Smith.

CHAPTER 6

Deputy Dawson stepped away from the corpse and to the edge of the yellow crime scene tape.

He'd gotten the call two hours ago, notified the coroner, and hurried to the remote site at Cedar Flute ruins. He'd taken dozens of photographs of the area and the body, at Dr. Richards's direction, then searched the man's pockets and bagged and tagged the contents. He continued to wear a pair of blue surgical gloves.

Students huddled in small groups a few yards away. They'd identified the dead man as archeology professor Jed Hollins and the driver's license confirmed it.

"Deputy?"

Dawson turned back to Dr. Richards and understood. Time to get the body into the body bag.

He helped position the heavy black sack, already laid open on the ground.

Don't look at his eyes. Though he'd been in law enforcement for nearly a decade, he'd seen only three dead bodies. Still, he'd learned not to stare at their eyes. Eyes were meant to see and swivel and squint with a smile, not turn all milky and vacant. Not to stare into darkness.

The coroner took Hollins's arms, Dawson his feet, and they slid, then rolled the man onto the rubberized bag. With some shifting and pulling, they got him fully into the bottom and the doctor zipped the container closed.

Dawson stood and pulled the gloves from his hands, the nastiest part of the job done for the day. With Sherriff Leavitt away at the Rural County Law Enforcement Conference, held this year in Tucson, Dawson was on his own until at least Friday.

"What can you tell me, doctor?"

Richards was a short, wiry man in his early fifties, hair tucked under a brown safari-style hat. "Suffocation, maybe."

Dawson squinted, seeking an explanation.

"Bluish lips, bloodshot eyes."

"Strangled?"

"Can't tell you that yet, deputy. No obvious marks on his head or neck. Have to complete the exam to tell you much more."

"Shit." All these students were potential suspects.

He was going to have to round them up on his own. Dawson thought for a moment. "Poison?"

"Not probable, but possible. I'll get the body to the morgue," Richards nodded, "if you'll help me get him in the cooler."

"That's not exactly a picnic cooler." Dawson pointed to the heavy, refrigerated van.

"But you can keep beer in it," Richards teased. The coroner's high-tech vehicle was the county's budget buster last year, a nod to law enforcement after commissioners decided the sheriff didn't need any more deputies than he already had—Dawson, on site, and Rowe, manning the office. The ruins abutted the eastern boundary of Canyonlands, just outside the national park. Since the death seemed to have occurred at the ruins, Dawson didn't expect much federal assistance.

They slid a canvas stretcher under the body bag and wrestled it into the refrigerated van.

"Let me know if you see any other vehicles on your way back to your office, will you?" Dawson asked. "Description and license plate numbers if you can."

"You bet."

"And where you saw them and which way they were going."

"Just on the dirt road?" The unpaved road ran for

twenty-seven miles before it intersected with asphalt.

"Yeah, good enough."

Dr. Richards hopped into the van and began a slow ride away from the pueblo ruins. Dawson pulled a yellow legal pad from his patrol car and a pen and walked several yards to the students. They gathered quickly around him as they sensed an announcement.

"Okay, we need to proceed in an orderly fashion."

Some students watched him closely, others held their heads low or seemed to be staring into space.

"Who found the body?"

Four hands went into the air.

"You folks please put your name and contact information on this pad." He handed it to the nearest student, a thin young man with blue eyes, stringy hair, and a stubble of a beard. "Include phone numbers, emails, physical address, full legal name, please."

He waited as they scribbled and passed the pad from one to the other, then he took the pad from the last student.

"Now, the rest of you, please sign in." He counted a total of nineteen students and would check the number of names on the list before he released them, to make sure someone didn't think they could avoid signing the list.

"You folks," he pointed to the four, "let's start with

the first person to find the professor. Who is that?"

The student with the stringy hair raised his hand.

"Your name?"

"Keith Simmons."

"Okay, Keith. Please step behind that boulder and I'll be right with you. The rest of you, please stay together and take a rest. Keep passing that pen and pad around. I'll get back to you as soon as I can."

Dawson followed the student around the large sandstone and verbally confirmed his name, status, name of the archeology course, and other details.

"Now tell me what you saw and how you found Professor Hollins."

The young man glanced at the ground, shifting his feet. "I came around the bend, just past the ruins, and there he was, lying on the ground."

"Anyone else there?"

"Yeah," he looked up at Dawson, his expression animated. "I saw a guy there, a man with black hair in a ponytail. And maybe a goatee."

Dawson felt a jolt of energy. He'd been looking for a man of that description for years, a hermit suspected of moonshining in the outback. The sightings were often in connection with archeological sites, kivas, and caches. Rumors spread that the recluse sold moonshine for cash but avoided nearly everyone, especially law enforcement.

No one seemed to have a name for this phantom or know why he had been at these places or where he'd gone when law enforcement arrived.

Dawson nodded at the student, urging him to say more.

"I yelled to him, 'Hey, you, stop,' but he just kinda looked at me. I thought he'd hurt the professor, though, so, well, I had my notebook and a shovel. I ran up to him and swung the shovel at him, to get him away from Professor Hollins. He dodged me the first time…" he mimicked the motion for Dawson. "Then I swung again, and he kicked me, made me fall to the ground on top of the professor." The student shook his head at the memory. "I thought I'd failed him—Professor Hollins—but later we felt for a pulse and realized he was already dead when I'd tried to defend him."

"Did you see this man hurt the professor?"

"Yeah, sure. Well…he was on the ground next to him, hand on his neck."

"His neck?"

"Yeah. He stood up when I ran at him."

"What happened after you were kicked to the ground?"

"It took me a few seconds to get back up, you

know. I had dropped the shovel, so I got it again, but the man was gone."

"Did you look for him?"

"Yeah, some. I mean I followed and looked around, but Will and Rob and Susan were behind me, and I heard them shouting about the professor, that he was dead. So I turned back and went to the professor, all of us there. Will felt for a pulse and said he couldn't find one."

"That's when someone called 911?"

"Rob went out into the open for a better signal and called, yeah."

Dawson rubbed his chin. The mystery man of the desert had just become murder suspect number one.

CHAPTER 7

Charles's question about the gauges had been weighing on Betty's mind. What if replacement pumps continued to get pressure readings below the required pounds per square inch? What did the low readings even mean? Failing pumps? At ten thousand dollars a pump, and twelve pumps, that would be one hell of a new expense, and just at the wrong time. A leak in the system? How expensive would replacement piping be? How long would they be shut down for repairs?

A block grant from Global Green Engineering was set for final approval in a few days. Transfer of funds to Sapphire Solutions was expected shortly after that. Fifty-five million dollars to expand the system and showcase the technology as a key component of the new president's ambitious environmental policy. Rather than reduce the use of fossil fuels to a trickle, the administration set about to improve on a practice developed in Iceland decades ago. Keep producing all the greenhouse gases you want, America, and let the newest engineering take care of it. The oil and gas industry loved it. And the industry quietly donated millions to Global Green Engineering to support the approach.

Now was not the time for those gauges to be acting up.

If new gauges continued to show low readings, that could delay and even prevent the funding altogether. They had big plans as soon as that money hit the Sapphire Solutions bank account. Her mind wandered to an image of her and Charles in beach chairs by the ocean, holding drinks with little umbrellas in them.

Stay focused.

Charles had said to have Dom and Parker replace the gauges. She'd liked Charles's idea to tap the talents of Mr. Smith, too. She'd seen him walk through the lobby this morning and asked to speak with him. Smith's contacts in industry were phenomenal, and for a reasonable price he'd agreed to provide the special replacement gauges she needed. If they solved the problem, she and Charles could be sitting on that beach in less than two weeks.

A knock on her door jarred her thoughts. She straightened her shirt. "Come in."

Dom slid into her office. They each nodded a greeting to the other and Dom sat in the chair across from her desk.

"Dom, I need you to make a trip for us." Betty rested her hands atop a thin report with a cover sheet marked "Confidential." "As you know, we have a pumping station about a three-hour drive from here, over in Utah. Moonshine Mesa. The old oil field at the edge of Smoky Dome."

Dom nodded. The "dome" was an underground reservoir of oil, shaped like an upside-down bowl, buried under tons of rock and earth. The oil field was on the western edge of the dome. As he recalled, they'd pumped a mixture of water, salts, and chemicals into the ground the last couple of years, squeezing oil through the geologic structure toward the well.

"Do you know where the station is?" she asked.

"Yeah, I've been to the Cedar Flute ruins, the pueblo ruins at the bottom of the mesa, along the river."

"Yes. The station is on top of the mesa. For some reason, we're getting pressure readings that aren't right—they don't make sense." She looked into his eyes. "Too low, mostly. We need you and Parker to go out there and replace the pressure gauges."

"When?"

"Tuesday, first thing. But it's a long drive out there, so start early. There's a house trailer there that's been unused for a while. There's electricity in it, of course, there mostly for the pumps, but I can't guarantee the condition of the trailer. You might be able to recharge your cell phone inside if you need to. There are two outhouses nearby, left there after the pumps were installed. You'll need to bring your own drinking water."

"Sure. Take my own vehicle?"

"Yes, I was hoping you still had your four wheel drive?"

She meant Dom's 1971 Bronco. "Yeah."

"Perfect. Most of the way is over rough road. The gauges are TR-317s and we've decided to replace them all. I've already ordered new ones that should arrive at your office late this afternoon. You can shut off the flow at the pumps, replace the gauges, then turn the flow back on, right?"

"You bet. I can test the old ones if you like and then if they're off base, I can replace them right then and there."

"No. We've got a deadline out there and decided to just replace the gauges. There are only four of them. The new ones will be tested to specifications before they deliver them to you."

"Do you have the specs on the pumps?"

"We have…" she hesitated.

"I can take those, too, in case I can see anything else not right." He pointed at the red-cover report in her hands.

"Not this." She slid it into the top drawer of her desk. "But I'll put what I have on your desk by the end of the day."

Dom's forehead wrinkled. "Okay…"

"For now, all we need you to do is replace the gauges." Dom could be a bit nosey, but he knew how to follow orders. "Bring the old ones back here to me. And let us know if you find anything that doesn't seem right. It's on a federal lease within the national park and really remote. Cell phone service is spotty in that area but there's some coverage right at the station. Call me when you arrive, when you're done, and when you are about to leave."

"Got it," Dom nodded.

Betty looked at the calendar on her desk. "Need anything else?"

"I guess not." Dom stood.

CHAPTER 8

Dawson thought Keith's story seemed credible and it was supported by statements from the other three students who had found the professor's body. Those three hadn't seen the man with the ponytail, but Keith had told them immediately that the mystery man had kicked him to the ground and run away.

Dawson believed him.

Close questioning established that none of the other students had seen anything suspicious, either before or after their discovery of the body. He would rather have asked all of them individually and privately, but he didn't have the time nor the manpower at that moment.

None of the students knew of anyone who would want to harm Professor Hollins or anyone whose behavior at the site was unusual.

With one exception.

When pressed, Keith said he wondered why one of

the students had left the site early, someone named Claire Lin. She'd left after Keith had found Hollins dead but before the deputy had arrived. He wondered, in particular, because of a rumor that she and Professor Hollins had been romantically involved. If true, it would be a source of strong feelings between the two of them. Something he needed to explore. And why had she driven her own vehicle all the way out here when she could have shared a ride with the other students?

Dawson had taken photographs of each of the students there and the university vehicles they'd driven to the site, then sent them back to their campus. He could confirm their names and contact information with the college registrar, so at least he would be dealing with a known number of potential suspects and witnesses, assuming there was anything else to suspect or witness.

He would follow up with private interviews about the professor and this Claire Lin and see if anyone there could have had a motive for killing him. The other deputy, Rowe, could help him with that until the sheriff got back.

Why would the ponytailed man strangle the professor? Did it have anything to do with the archeological site? The restoration of part of the ruins? Or was there some kind of campus-related reason? A jealous lover?

The autopsy would take another few days, but the death could not have been accidental, could it?

Maybe he should brief Deputy Rowe and let her handle all the follow up interviews. Somebody had to try to track down the man with the ponytail. The only witness, or maybe even the perpetrator, was someone he had to find and confront.

Just beyond the ruins lay the border for Canyonlands National Park. So the site of the crime, if there was one, was squarely in the county—the sheriff's jurisdiction. But the ponytailed man seemed to have fled into federal territory. He'd notify the park service that he was going to search. He doubted they'd have the manpower to help right away; their rangers were spread far and wide. But the man's footprints would disappear entirely if he waited too long.

Finding the mystery man was up to him.

Dawson set his pad of paper under a rock and began to search for footprints leading away from where the professor had died. Camera in hand, he circled a large boulder in the direction the student said the ponytailed man had fled. After a few minutes, he found a clear print moving away from the area, down toward a side canyon that fed into the Colorado River.

Dawson snapped a few photographs of the boot

prints and followed them, glancing around from time to time to keep his bearings. He passed a dead crow along the way. He lost the trail for a bit, then recovered it as the prints led into the side canyon, a deep, narrow crevasse carved from the plateau above by an intermittent stream. He followed partial footprints deeper into the slot canyon. Sandstone walls rose hundreds of feet above him, pressing him more and more tightly between them. When the cliffs became only fifteen feet apart, Dawson drew his pistol. There could be no way out of this canyon except the way he was walking in. The man could be lying in ambush.

The deputy moved more slowly, scanning the ledges above as he walked. The canyon bent to his right and narrowed a bit more. A few yards deeper in, he reached a jumble of scree at the base of the cliffs. Theoretically, a hiker could walk a little farther into the canyon, but it led to a dead end.

Silence seemed to press upon his ears, a heavy stillness in the air. He looked up, down, back the way he'd come, everywhere he could, but saw nothing but jagged cliffs reaching for the desert sky.

He relaxed and holstered his gun.

The boot prints he'd followed ended in the rocky scree but the cliff above was sheer and imposing.

The man had to have climbed upward, but a free-style ascent would be dangerous. He might have used a rope, which probably meant he'd arrived in this canyon by rappelling down the canyon walls and gone back up using the same rope.

Why had he come down the cliff face here? Why had he then hiked to Cedar Flute? Though farther to travel, there was a well-worn trail south of the ruins. There was even a pump station on top of the plateau with dirt road access a few miles to the east. Easier ways, by far, to get to the Cedar Flute site.

And, of course, why had the man run away?

Whatever the answers might be, Dawson was not going to find them standing here.

CHAPTER 9

Dom's fingers dangled from the metal rim; his wrist pushed against the top of the old steering wheel. He seemed to navigate down the dusty road without effort, weaving gently to avoid a rock here and there, but his eyes pulled tightly in concern.

"What're you thinking about, Dom?" Parker squeezed the armrest as they dodged a rough patch in the gravel.

Dom glanced sideways at him and frowned. "I can't help wondering why we're the ones all the way out here just to swap out a couple of pressure gauges. Be easier to find somebody local to do it."

"Gets us out of the office." Parker shrugged and looked out his window. "We're way the hell out here, though."

They'd left the city at six o'clock that morning and traveled down the highway into Utah. Two hours later, they'd taken a turn onto the unpaved road, gravel in places, bare dirt in others. They'd crossed into Canyonlands National Park and driven nearly an hour on this route. Dom occasionally checked a hand-written map on the front seat next to him, telling Parker he didn't trust satellite-based maps in the back country, assuring him that the gods at Google didn't always know where you actually wanted to go.

"Should be there soon," Dom said.

"Where are we now, exactly?" Parker pointed ahead at the sage and grass covered plateau. Small cedars dotted a landscape otherwise barren of trees. For a time, they could see an edge to the flats where a gorge had formed, then they'd turned west, away from the cliffs.

"We're on Moonshine Mesa, at the corner of No and Where." Dom put both hands on the steering wheel.

"How did the mesa get that name?"

"There used to be a couple of springs up here somewhere. Prohibition ran from the 1920s to the early 30s. Moonshiners had some stills out here, keeping the townspeople loose and happy."

"And the revenuers busy, I'd guess."

They dipped a few feet below ground level, rose up a small hill, and leapt over the top, gravity neutralized for a millisecond. Electric poles appeared on their right and, when the road turned that same direction, they suddenly saw rows of pewter-colored rectangles, each the size of a child's bedroom, wires reaching between them like tentacles. Gadgets and vents and bulges sat atop each one, reminding him of old-time, steam-powered train engines. Parker had no idea what these ones were for.

A red fuel tank perched on iron stilts above an engine the size of a farm tractor—some kind of back-up generator for the electric grid.

Dom lifted his foot from the gas pedal, letting the Bronco coast onto the flattened area near the pumps. Farther to their right stood a battered house trailer, balding tires laid out atop its roof to help keep it from blowing away. The skirt along the bottom was missing two front panels, holes in its yellowed teeth. A couple of fiberglass porta-johns sat to the side of the trailer, their tops sunburned to a translucent shade of beige.

"This is it." Dom glanced at his hand-drawn map and brought them to a stop.

It took a moment for the rumble of the road to fade from Parker's ears.

They stretched their legs and took long drinks of water before opening the rear of the Bronco and pulling out the new gauges. Dom carried his toolbox and told Parker to bring one of the units, and they walked to the gray pumps, feeling the electric hum rising from their toes.

Dom led them through the machinery to a spot where a pressure gauge was attached to a pipeline. A thin wire held a lever in place below the line to keep it from being raised accidentally.

"1,065 psi." Dom pointed to the old gauge. "I guess that's lower than it should be. Lower than what they want." He removed the wire and pushed the lever from a downward position to an upward one and the needle dropped to zero.

"How does all this work?" Parker swept his arm toward the pumps.

"When oil fields were first running, there was plenty of underground pressure to push oil to the surface. As they depleted, companies injected the wells with water or chemical fluids in one place to push the oil out at another place. But I'm not sure what's going on here, exactly..." Dom pulled a wrench from his tools and carefully twisted the gauge until it seemed to break free, then unwound it from the threads.

Parker handed him a new gauge, painted bright blue on the back, but Dom stopped to stare at it. The needle read 2,100 psi.

"Something's not right here," Dom tapped the

glass cover and shook it, but the needle stayed where it was. "It should read zero when it's not hooked up. This damn thing is crooked."

"What?"

"It shouldn't be stuck where it is. Grab me another one, will you?"

Parker nodded and trotted back to the pale blue Bronco.

They examined another gauge, also stuck on 2,100 psi. Parker made another trip and they found that all four of the new gauges were set at that reading.

"Could they just be at that pressure to start with?" Parker asked. "Maybe they work just fine once actual pressure is on each of them. Maybe the needle is just set there as a default or something."

"Doesn't make sense to me, but let's see what happens." Dom installed a new gauge on the line and pushed the lever back to its original position. The needle wobbled a bit, then settled in near 2,100 psi.

"Let's disconnect it and see if it goes to zero." Dom repeated the process and pulled the new gauge from the pipe.

The needle moved downward, but not below 2,050 psi.

"This should read zero when the pressure's turned

off. These things are crap. Or they've been tampered with." Dom set the blue-backed gauge on the ground. "I'm calling Betty."

They stepped beyond the large pumps and walked toward the trailer house. Dom pulled his cell phone from his pocket and dialed.

"Hey, this is Dom. I'm looking for Betty…When? No, I need to talk to her now…Uh, huh. No, well, sure." He covered the phone with his hand and said to Parker, "Figures. No Betty today. Going to try Mr. Story."

Parker nodded.

"Yes? No, Cindy. Well, are you sure? Of course, he's in court all day," he said with a hint of sarcasm. "All right then, we couldn't reach Betty, so we thought we'd try him. It's okay. No, no message. We'll be back in the office tomorrow."

"No luck?"

"Jackasses, the lot of them," Dom hung up and put his phone away.

"That's a little harsh, isn't it?" Parker tried to get Dom to look him in the eye.

"You don't know these people the way I do. This is just typical. They'll send us off on an errand that can't be done then complain when it's not been done."

"Well, Mr. Story didn't send us here. He and Cindy wouldn't even know about this, would they?"

Dom looked at Parker from under his brow.

"Really. I mean, Betty wouldn't know these new gauges are messed up, either."

"Why are you defending her?"

"I'm not. I mean, I am, but…"

"But?" Dom put his fists on his hips.

"Hey, you've been here for years, but I'm the new guy. I'm just trying to fit in here."

"This is not some crush on Cindy…"

"No. I mean, not all of it." He glanced at the ground then back at Dom. "Hey, I'm making some progress with Betty and some of the others."

"Yeah?"

"Look, Dom. To be honest about it, I just don't seem to fit in very well in general. I'd really like to be part of a team, you know?"

Dom lowered his hands and unclenched them. He turned toward the trailer and shook his head. "Yeah, yeah. I get it."

"You're not pissed at me?"

"No." he turned back to Parker. "This isn't really about you. This is about Betty and these gauges. And the fact that I can't reach her to ask her about it. All day today. And after she insists that we call her when we're here."

"We'll just tell them when we get back."

"Something's up, I tell you. I don't trust Betty or her friends."

"What could possibly be up?"

"Look. She blamed me for a huge over-order of ceiling lights a few years ago and the company we'd gotten them from went out of business. We couldn't return any of the fixtures. She'd screwed up the order then lied to Charles and the others about it. Almost got me fired. I haven't trusted her ever since."

"Oh…"

Dom's forehead creased, eyes on the ground, lips tightly pressed. He turned and marched toward a set of tubes that rose from the ground. Parker followed.

Dom examined the pipes, following an arrow that seemed to indicate the flow of liquid to the pumps. He stopped for a moment, rubbing his chin, then hurried to another set of pipes that paralleled the first set.

"Ha!"

"What?" Parker followed him.

"See those pipes?" Dom pointed behind him.

"Yeah…"

"Those are the right size, I think, for the water injection."

"Water?"

"A saline solution or water mixed with chemicals. Think of grease-cutting detergents. Like I said, the pumps create a hydraulic pressure—the injection pushes the oil out."

"Okay."

"But these," he pointed to the other set of pipes, "are the ones in use now and they're a different size…"

"So?"

"So, what's in them? See, the larger pipes have been shut off. What's in these smaller ones and why are they pumping it into the ground?"

"Isn't the field still producing oil? Maybe it's just a different solution, a different mix of stuff…"

"I don't think so. I mean, I'm not a petroleum engineer or anything, but it doesn't look like it to me. It looks like they're pumping something into the ground, but nothing is coming out. See over there?" he pointed. "No oil is shown as moving though the downhill pipeline. It's like they want to store something in there, without pushing out any oil."

"The oil is all gone?"

"Looks like it, or they'd be sending it through the pipeline toward a refinery. And the new gauges they want us to put in read a much higher pressure than the ones that are installed now."

"Why would they do that?"

"Betty had better have a damn good answer."

CHAPTER 10

Leaving the old moonshiner's camp behind, Relic headed out across the plateau, searching for the route he'd taken earlier. After nearly a half mile, he found two of his boot prints and one of the dead bees still lying next to them.

He knelt and examined the insect again, lifting him gently by the wings. The tiny body was fully intact and, aside from being dead, did not appear to be injured.

"What did this to you?" he asked, replacing the bee on the sand near a jagged crack in the sandstone bed. He stood and scanned the area. From a distance, or from the air, the plateau appeared to be flat and smooth, small evergreens spread haphazardly across the surface. But at ground level, the plateau rose and fell in swells that displayed large swaths of land or hid them from view. Outcrops of rock bulged from under the surface, bare knuckles rising through fists of dirt. Grass tangled like tufts of hair on weathered skin, junipers twisted by desert wind into gnarled, hoary sentinels.

A shallow drainage wound to his left, toward the northeast, and he slid into the arroyo and resumed his trek, watching for more dead bees—or live ones for that matter—anything that might help him understand the string of death he'd come across. He walked for two miles without finding anything else of special interest when the drainage dropped into a wider, deeper ravine that ran more northerly and southerly. He chose to move south, away from the deeper canyons, along a winding path about forty feet wide and twelve feet below the surface of the plateau. Outcrops of sandstone forced spring rains into sharp corners, gouging the earth into muddy channels on the opposite side. Driftwood had piled against a ledge just above his head, trapped there after a minor flood.

The ground above him became rockier as he hiked, shelves of stone stacked atop each other into uneven cliffs. Shadows filled the arroyo as the sun dropped behind him, cooling the air.

Still no other dead bees. Or crows. Or anything else.

A musky odor wafted through the ravine, and suddenly the air seemed to fill with a static charge, an electric energy that made him stop mid-step. His skin tensed and tingled, tiny hairs on his neck rising. He sniffed, but the scent had vanished with the breeze.

Something was in the arroyo with him. He searched the ledge above him, the drainage behind him, the places something could hide, and just then he realized what it was.

Relic walked slowly backward, keeping his gaze ahead but moving his eyes across the walls of the ravine. He moved toward the wood that had caught on an outcrop behind him and pulled the knife from his sheath. When he reached the driftwood, he slid his pack onto the ground and pulled sticks from the bundle, always watching ahead of him. When he had enough wood, he carved shavings from a larger stick, stacked them with small twigs on the ground, and reached for his matches.

Something shifted ahead of him.

He bent close to the shavings, blowing on them to get his fire started. In moments, the dry wood broke into flame and he leaned more wood onto the blaze. He pulled another stick from the pile, nearly as thick and long as his arm, and placed the smallest end into the fire.

Smoke rose in the shifting air and spread above the edge of the ravine like a thin fog. He waited for the wood to burn hotter and put his pack back on. Holding the knife in his left hand, he grabbed the long stick from the fire, careful to keep it alight.

A low-throated rumble seemed to levitate from the cliffs. The smell of smoke was changing the equation between them. It created a danger, frustrating her plans.

His pulse quickened.

She was out there, waiting for him, hunting him. Maybe she'd tracked him into the gorge and moved ahead for an ambush. It was exactly what he would have done.

He stomped the little fire into embers and moved along the rock wall opposite the side he knew she'd be, carrying the blazing stick in front of him as he went.

Avoiding this confrontation would only prolong it.

One of them had to back off, and it wasn't going to be him.

CHAPTER 11

Dawson spread a topographical map across the table, an abstract representation of the earth based on elevations on the ground. Brown contour lines squiggled across the plateau in random curves that roughly paralleled other curves, one within the other, to the highest point in any given area. Wider regions were outlined in shapes with no apparent pattern at all; Rorschach stains outlined in ink. Canyons, where the cliffs were especially steep, showed marks so close together they seemed to have no separation at all.

He pulled another map from the shelf and positioned it next to the first, showing an expanded area. On the eastern corner of the second map were the Cedar Flute ruins. The slot canyon where he'd tracked the ponytail man was just north of that, upstream from the Colorado River. Farther east, onto the main map, the canyon reached its dead end. North and east of that was a high plateau, the map confirming that the area was marked by arroyos, knolls, and rocky outcrops.

On the eastern end of the main map was a boxed-in area noted as an oil field and pumping station. A dirt road led to the station, its origins off the end of the map but presumably leading to a paved road. Behind the pumps was a steep cliff that dropped to a canyon running west and north, but Dawson knew that it eventually turned south to drain into the Colorado River.

He ran his finger along the slot canyon and across the plateau. If the ponytail man had continued east, he might be going to the oil field. Dawson could begin his search from there and head west, hoping to intercept him.

Of course, if the man had gone straight north, he could be anywhere by now. If he'd gone south? He shifted the maps across the table. The man had climbing gear, that much was clear. If he'd gone south, he could rappel down a large canyon below the ruins and make his way back to them. But it seemed unlikely that he would return to where he'd killed the professor. If that was what had happened.

Dawson could drive to the pump station and hike west from there, crisscrossing the mesa for signs of the ponytail man. That seemed like his best option, though he knew it was a long shot. Sheriff Leavitt was still at his convention in Tucson, so Dawson didn't need to ask permission. He suspected that if he had to ask, Leavitt would say no. The sheriff was always ready to let the feds take the lead. Any case potentially involving federal lands got the same, quick response from Leavitt: let the park rangers or the FBI handle it.

Deputy Rowe walked into the conference room and nodded at Dawson. Only one year out of the academy, Rowe was young but sharp. Whenever Sheriff Leavitt and Dawson were out, she'd been staffing the office and dealing with the usual string of complaints and problems by herself. She wore a disarming smile but was tough as rawhide, a country girl homemade for rural law enforcement. She looked at the topographic maps and grimaced.

"Yeah, tomorrow I'm going to take a shot at finding our missing man." Dawson pointed at the slot canyon where the man had disappeared. "He's our only real suspect. Or at least, he's a material witness."

"But…" Rowe waved her arm over the table.

"Yeah, I know, needle in a haystack. But if he went east, there's a decent chance of intercepting him from the west. He's got to go somewhere. And the nearest place to keep a vehicle, other than at the ruins, is this pumping station," he pointed. "The man may have a truck stashed there."

"We didn't find any vehicles at the ruins that weren't accounted for. And there aren't any out there now."

"Right. So, the next best possibility is the pumping station. Sorry to leave you on your own again, but I'll kick myself if I don't take a shot at this."

"Why don't you take the drone with you," Rowe nodded. "It's in the garage."

"It's busted, remember?"

"Oh, right. Hey, I came in to tell you Dr. Richards just called."

Dawson straightened. "The autopsy?"

"Yep. Asphyxiation. Hypoxemia noted."

"But how? There were no bruises or marks on his neck, nothing covering his face…"

"I know," Rowe interrupted. "The doc is puzzled by it, too. But he's absolutely certain that's how Professor Hollins died."

Dawson pinched the bridge of his nose.

CHAPTER 12

Relic moved slowly, ever so slowly, down the arroyo, keeping the burning branch ahead of him, spreading the smoke, skywriting figure eights as he went. He heard nothing but the crunch of his boots on gravel as he rounded a curve in the drainage.

He stopped and held his breath.

There she crouched, about forty yards away and six feet higher than where he stood. The cougar stared at him, eyes blank and glassy, nose twitching at the scent of the burning wood.

They stared at each other for several moments, then she rose casually and looked away, transformed into an innocent house cat, her deadly essence hidden in an air of indifference. Watching where she placed her feet, she padded in absolute silence up the ledge and onto the plateau above.

She flicked her tail as she disappeared.

His arms relaxed a notch.

He'd won this round—he'd scared her off. Her ambush had been foiled and she knew it. She wouldn't try again right away, but he wondered what made her try at all. Mountain lions usually hunted prey that were smaller and less dangerous than adult humans. Was she ill? Did she have cubs to protect? Or had she been waiting on another animal when he appeared instead?

He kept the long stick burning but quickened his pace up the arroyo, searching for an easy place to climb out. When he found one, he looked around again and snuffed out the fire in a patch of sand. He rose onto higher ground and hiked to the east, away from the predacious cat.

Sagebrush slowed his progress, but he kept a steady pace toward an outcrop of sandstone about a mile away. A brassy sun glared behind him, warming the rocks and slinging shadows across the landscape.

The outcrop stood about eight feet high, sandstone carved by eons of wind and rain into a natural shelter under a cap of stone. Relic put the burnt stick and his pack on the ground at the rear of the carved-out rock. He pulled his knife and went looking for more wood. The sun soon touched the horizon, plasma flares burning the cotton bottoms of plumped-up clouds.

He carried an armload of wood back to the shelter and set out to the east for more. An oil field and pump station were in the area. He would need water tomorrow and there might be a well or reservoir there he could use. If not, he could try digging into sand in the arroyo and collecting water that way.

The ground rose gently as he went, and when he reached the crest, he could see boxy, metal shapes flashing in the last rays of light.

CHAPTER 13

They'd left the pump station yesterday evening and driven through the night to return home. Dom dropped him off at his apartment, where Parker had leftover sausage and beans, then played Plants vs Zombies on his virtual reality goggles. He'd slept fitfully and had a hot shower and two cups of coffee the next morning to get himself in gear. He'd forgotten to recharge his cell phone overnight, but he could do that at work.

Dom was waiting for him when he arrived.

"Good morning." Parker walked to a chair across from Dom's desk and sat.

"Humph." Dom's eyes were tense and grim. "Ready to go see Betty?" Dom forced the words through tightened lips.

Parker swallowed. "Batten down the hatches?"

"Yep." Dom marched out of his office and onto the terrazzo lobby, Parker in tow. They knocked at Betty's office and, when no one replied, Dom went inside and motioned Parker to close the door behind them.

"She's not here…"

"I can see that." Dom moved behind Betty's desk and opened the drawer on the left. He rummaged through something and pulled out a folder with a red cover on top marked as confidential. "Here it is. I saw her with this yesterday and wondered about it."

Dom sat in Betty's chair and began reading the report.

Parker looked around the room. "Are you sure it's OK—"

"Hang on," Dom interrupted, scanning the pages.

Parker could hear a distant ding at the elevator across the lobby. People were coming and going, a busy morning beginning to find its pace.

"Listen to this…" Dom began, running a finger under words on the page. "Global Green Engineering has granted fifty-five million dollars to Solar Gem for some sort of carbon project near Smoky Dome. And the transfer of funds is scheduled for the end of next week."

"What does that have to do with the broken gauges?" Parker said.

"I don't know yet…" He turned another page. "But Solar Gem is coming into a massive payday. Wait…"

Dom turned a few more pages.

Parker opened the office door a crack and peeked outside.

"Hey, here it is… references to storage."

"Not to be too blunt, but so what?" Parker could see a couple of people crossing the lobby to reach the elevators. He closed the door again.

"Yeah…" Dom scratched between his eyes. "And what is this Solar Gem company?"

"Why would Betty—the property manager—have those papers?" Parker asked.

"It must be a corporate client."

"Then it should be in an attorney's office." Parker pointed at the file.

Dom looked up at Parker. "Yeah, you're right." He leafed through the documents again, blue eyes searching closely.

Parker rocked back on his heels, wishing Dom would hurry up.

"Hey, look at this!" Dom waved a page in the air. "Sapphire Solutions is the parent company for Solar Gem. And the CFO of Solar Gem is none other than our lovely Betty Coulter." He tore three pages from the report and folded them into his back pocket.

CHAPTER 14

"Things are pretty hectic right now." Dawson set down his phone and put it on speaker. "Rowe's busy out at the McCullum Ranch and our front desk has been fielding all the calls."

"You need to stay there for a while," Sheriff Leavitt began.

"Uh-huh," Dawson mumbled, not wanting to agree to the command. He was planning to drive to the pump station today and begin a search for the ponytail man.

"I had a call about twenty minutes ago from Dr. Sanchez, president of the university where the dead man taught. He's coming to see you with some of his staff."

Oh, great. "When?"

"Right now."

"Crap."

"Dawson?"

"Sorry, sir, it's just that I'm really jammed up right now."

"Well, un-jam yourself for a meeting with folks who are legitimately concerned about the progress of our investigation. Not to mention influential members of the community. You've got to assure them there was no foul play involved. Though a bit unusual, it seems to have been a natural death."

"What about the mystery man our witness saw? The student who found Professor Hollins saw someone touching Hollins's neck, hovering over him. And he ran when confronted—"

"I know you're worried about that, Dawson, but there were no signs of struggle on the body. This so-called mystery man is a witness, but we can't conclude he was a killer."

Dawson was convinced the missing man was involved in the professor's death. Sheriff Leavitt wanted to clip his investigation short.

"Right, Dawson?"

"I understand what you're saying."

"Right."

Dawson clenched his fists. If he wasn't careful here, the sheriff would order him not to conduct any further searches for the ponytail man. He would write off Hollins's death as natural and drop any further investigation.

Dawson heard a knock on the door. Grace, the sheriff's long-time communications officer, leaned into the room.

"Some people from the university are here to see you, deputy." She slid her glasses higher on her nose and gave him a half-grimace that apologized for the intrusion.

"Yes, Sheriff Leavitt's on the speaker," he pointed to his cell phone. "I'll be with them in just a minute."

She nodded and pulled the door closed behind her.

"Just listen to them, Dawson. Assure them we're doing all we can," Leavitt said.

Except pulling out all the stops to find the pony-tailed man. "Of course, sir. Talk with you later."

"Copy that."

Dawson hung up the call, straightened his duty belt, and opened the door. A pencil-thin man with gray, receding hair, a dark jacket, and no tie approached Dawson and offered his hand. He introduced himself as President Sanchez and his two associates as professors at the university. Professor Sonders, head of the archeology department, wore a deep frown, her nose a pinch of skin between narrow eyes. Professor Kelce, head of the history department, seemed to have a mild bowel obstruction, his lips a tight and slightly crooked line, his hands clasping each other in a death grip.

"Professors, please come in." Dawson waved them into his office.

Sanchez jumped right to the point. "Your staff explained that Sheriff Leavitt is out of town. We're here to see what you can tell us about the investigation, deputy."

Dawson closed his door and pointed to the chairs in front of his desk. "Make yourselves comfortable."

His guests sat reluctantly, as if resting might relieve a pain they sought to relish.

"Thank you, deputy," Sanchez sat in a chair in front of Dawson's phone. Kelce stared at a sharpshooter's award on Dawson's wall. Sonders focused on a used artillery shell on Dawson's desk, used as a paperweight.

"I understand that you spoke with the sheriff yesterday?" Dawson asked.

"Yes," Sanchez said.

"I don't know if there's much more I can tell you. The coroner has concluded that your Professor Hollins died of asphyxiation."

Professor Sonders seemed to twitch.

"I am very sorry for your loss," Dawson continued. "We're doing all we can to figure out what happened out there."

"The Cedar Flute complex is a very important site,

deputy." Professor Sonders raised her finger in the air. "It appears to have been a key location for exchanges and developments in pottery patterns and techniques. The artifacts connect a fascinating migration pattern that spreads across all of the southwest. And, of course, the flute that gave the site its name is an invaluable find. Our reconstruction work there has been top-notch; not something we want to abandon. We have two courses focused on the site as an archeological case study and two more planned for next year."

"Yes?" Dawson folded his hands together, a gesture meant to help slow his own thoughts and improve his show of patience.

"Well, you can imagine the angst we're all suffering. Of course, his close friends and family are suffering, but the department is, too. The archeology department must continue its vital work." Sonders nodded, agreeing with herself.

These folks are not grieving, Dawson thought. Did they dislike Professor Hollins? Were they glad he was no longer among the living?

"If the site is not safe for us," Kelce glanced at his colleagues, "or for our students, then we must engage in a massive and expensive course-correction. No pun intended."

"Let me say," Professor Sonders leaned forward, "that we absolutely must know whether this was a natural death or not. If not, we cannot expose ourselves or our students or benefactors to any kind of risk."

"Yes." Dawson thought for a moment. "Our office has not reached any final conclusion about that. But Sheriff Leavitt believes it must have been by natural causes. Not to be too graphic here, but Professor Hollins had no wounds of any kind on his body. No defensive wounds, which could suggest an attack. No bruising, no cuts or unusual scratches. He suffocated, but there's no apparent reason for it. At least, I should say, no nefarious reason."

"That's not much of an assurance, deputy," said Sanchez.

Dawson took a breath. "I must ask you folks, since you are here, whether any of you know of anyone who would have wanted to kill Professor Hollins."

"No, of course not," Sanchez said.

"Was there anyone in his life who was angry with him, upset about anything he'd done?"

They all shook their heads.

"Nothing on campus that might have raised anger against him?"

"Not that we know of," Sanchez said.

"No…professional jealousies?" Dawson watched them from under his brow.

"You're not saying that someone on the university staff was behind this?" Kelce stuttered.

"I'm not saying anything definitive, professor. But you folks seem to suggest that he was murdered. There must be some reason for your concern."

"I've suggested no such thing," Sanchez stood. "Our concern is for the safety of our students."

Dawson stayed in his seat.

"Indeed," Sanchez said.

Kelce and Sonders stood.

"Please let me know if any of you think of why anyone on campus would have wanted Professor Hollins dead." Dawson rose slowly.

"Oh," Kelce's voice expelled with a puff of air.

"I don't think I like your insinuation." Sanchez's eyes tightened into slits.

"That's just fine. We all have our jobs to do." Dawson's grin let them know that he was not perturbed by their discomfort.

The professors turned in unison and marched out of his office.

He plopped back into his chair.

Well, he'd screwed that one up for Sheriff Leavitt

about as much as anyone could have.

CHAPTER 15

Betty marched into her office. "What the hell do you think you're doing!?" Her fists clenched and her cheeks flushed.

Parker took a step back.

Dom stood from behind her desk, tossing the confidential report onto the top of her "out" box. "That's exactly what I wanna know."

"Get away from my desk." She glanced at the document and sucked a deep breath of air. "That's none of your business, Dom, and you know it!"

"You sent us all the way out there to fix those gauges—"

"Which you've obviously failed to do," she interrupted, stepping closer to her desk.

"…and it was just a wild goose chase. Dollars to dimes, the gauges out there are working just fine."

Her nostrils flared and her lips tightened like she'd just had a whiff of something terrible. "Bullshit."

Parker couldn't believe how fast her fury had ignited.

Dom moved to the side. "The new ones you gave us? They're crooked. They're set to the same psi that the report says is what you want those pumps to read."

Betty slid to the other side of her desk, maneuvering to get behind it and to force Dom away. "You don't have a clue what that project is all about!"

"It's not honest, I know that much." Dom circled to the front of the desk, relinquishing his ground but not his argument. "Those new gauges are fixed, Betty. Set to stay at the optimum pressure reading. They're not showing the true psi, so what are you hiding?"

Betty's eyes looked bloodshot now, her mouth in a snarl, red lipstick exaggerating the effect, and she seemed to have become a much older woman.

Dom leaned toward her. "I know about your big payday and that you two control the so-called Solar Gem company. So, what are you and Charles hiding? Why are you afraid of getting the true pressure readings on those pumps?"

She moved closer to Dom, her words crackling like summer grass on fire. "We're not hiding anything and we're not afraid of anything, you low-life piece of shit."

Parker's arms froze at his side. These two were ready for battle, right there and then.

"Hey, guys—" Parker tried to interject.

"Next time you need someone to do your dirty work, do it yourself!" Dom pointed his finger at her chest.

"Touch me and security will carry you out of here on a stretcher!"

"Hey, guys—"

"I wouldn't touch you with a ten-foot pole." Dom turned, stepped next to Parker, and folded his arms across his chest.

"I'm calling security. Rodney will toss your ass out of here." She lifted the phone on her desk.

"It will take a helluva lot more than Rodney," Dom declared, and something registered on her face, the red lips slackened, a quick acknowledgment of sorts. Or maybe an idea.

"Get out of my office! Now!" She pointed toward the door.

Dom glanced at Parker and nodded. "You haven't heard the last of this, Betty. Not by a long shot."

Dom spun and left the room. A split second later, Parker followed him out.

CHAPTER 16

Parker stayed behind Dom, thinking about what had just happened, replaying it again in his mind. They reached Dom's office and closed the door behind them.

"Couldn't there be some reason those gauges were tampered with? Some reasonable explanation?"

"You don't know Betty the way I do." Dom moved to the storage closet and pulled an empty box from the shelf. "Be careful around her and her cronies."

Parker moved to Dom's desk and sat in the chair across from it. "What are you going to do?"

"I'm figuring that out, but in the meantime, I'm done with this place."

Parker felt his stomach drop.

Dom walked to the wall and removed his swimsuit calendar, placing it in the bottom of the box.

"Hey, Dom, talk to me. What are you doing?"

"What I should have done last year."

"What?"

"Retiring."

Parker stood up.

Dom placed his bobble-doll hula dancer into the box and began rooting through his desk drawers, pulling items out and adding them to his collection of personal things.

"No, Dom, you can't. I can't do this job without you…"

"You can," Dom looked him in the eye. "You're a smart kid, Parker. You've seen my routine. You can pick up where I left off, no problem."

"I don't want you to leave," Parker's voice tumbled over something sharp, like it had tripped on a wire.

"It's OK." Dom touched Parker's shoulder. "You need this job. Just tell Betty you didn't understand what the big deal was. That I was off my rocker. Just keep your head down and you'll be fine."

"I…"

"You can do it." Dom reached into his back pocket. "And take this." He handed Parker the pages he'd removed from the report in Betty's desk.

"No…"

"Think of it as insurance, Parker. Just…tell them you never got to read it. Tell them I ran off with it. But you should put it someplace safe." Dom opened another drawer and began searching its contents.

Parker stood there, a numbness rising from his toes. Unsure what to do with the pages, he tucked them into his pants pocket.

"Hey, I left my small, red toolbox by the iron stairs in the auditorium. The little one with the socket wrenches?" Dom glanced at him. "Those are my personal tools. Would you go and get them for me?"

"Uh, sure." He still couldn't believe this was happening. "By the wall-ladder?"

"Yeah. Please."

"Sure, Dom." He stayed for a moment then turned and left the office, making his way to the auditorium.

This was a terrible development. He relied on Dom. He liked him. He was still learning the job. Now, what was he supposed to do? And if Betty was up to something shady, he wanted no part of it.

And what was Dom going to do about her?

Parker slid through the heavy double doors and searched the floor for the toolbox, looking under the theater-style seats as he made his way along the back row. He spotted the tools next to the velvet curtains, by the ladder that led to the ceiling fixtures. He grabbed them and hurried back through the doors.

Heels clacked against the terrazzo like castanets. He stopped at a corner wall, just beyond the auditorium, and peered around it.

Betty strode across the foyer toward the elevator, each step a purposeful strike against the polished floor.

He pulled back behind the wall and listened as the staccato faded away.

Coward.

He straightened his spine, determined to meet her face to face at the next opportunity. He hurried around the corner and toward Dom's office.

The door was ajar, so he pushed it open and stepped inside.

"Found it." He lifted the toolbox in the air, but Dom was not in the room. He placed the tools on Dom's desk and stared at the blank square on the wall where his calendar had been.

A man in a gray, button-down sweater stepped out of the storage closet on the back side of the office, his cheeks sunken like his skull had hollowed out beneath his eyes.

He raised a pistol and pointed it toward Parker's chest.

CHAPTER 17

A spark flashed down Parker's brainstem, a clutch-popping jar, torquing his hips, thighs, feet, tensing to flee. He turned and bent at the waist, pumping his legs into the tiled floor, propelling himself out of the office and into the lobby toward the auditorium, expecting a gunshot, listening, listening, but hearing none. Instantly out of breath, he gasped for air as his shoes squealed across the terrazzo and he crashed into the heavy theater doors, pulled one open, and slid inside.

He ran to the velvet curtains, spinning into a cocoon behind them, and reached for the rod-iron ladder that led to the ceiling. He glanced above and began stepping up the built-in rungs, trying not to jostle the curtains around him. Trying not to think about guns or agoraphobia.

He reached the top and lifted the panel, sliding it into the crawl space above the ceiling. He pulled himself into the space and slid to the side. Below, he could see the red curtains wave ever so slowly, disturbed by his ascent.

The heavy auditorium door banged open.

Parker placed the panel back over the entry as quietly as he could. He tried to slow his breathing but without much success. He crawled onto a row of three pine boards that rested on the metal frame of the ceiling. The boards led outward, maze-like, toward the backside of each of the light fixtures, all across the large theater. This was where Dom went to change the light bulbs. If he slipped off these boards, he would punch through the flimsy panels and crash into the seats below.

He lay next to the nearest fixture and forced himself to stop moving, stop making any noise at all. He took slow, deep breaths, finally getting enough oxygen.

He placed his right ear against the wooden flooring, listening as intently as he could. This was no virtual reality, no game of Plants vs Zombies. He smelled his own foul sweat, fear seeping from deep in his chest and through the pores in his skin.

Someone bumped against a row of chairs below him, feet shuffling down the theater aisle.

Who was that guy? If the man down there hadn't noticed the metal rungs behind the curtain, Parker had a chance. The thought helped him slow his heart.

Faint, scratching sounds faded away then increased in volume again, steps sliding across the carpet below. They seemed to stop directly underneath him.

All Parker could hear now was the thump of his heart, the rasp of air through his throat. The wait seemed to stretch into hours.

Then, slight movement and the loud clunks of the auditorium door as it opened and closed.

His body relaxed, melting into the floor, exhausted. He waited to make sure the door was not opened and closed as a trick, a diversion.

What the hell was going on? And where was Dom?

He counted one hundred seconds, then did it again.

Could he call 911 from up here? He patted his pants for his cell phone, then remembered he'd forgotten to charge the battery. He could retrace his steps back to Dom's office, but the man with the gun could still be there. He'd have to get help from someone in the building.

Betty? No. Dom didn't trust her and, after her display of anger earlier, he wasn't sure about her, either.

He could go to Cindy, up the back staircase. She could call 911 and he could tell them what he'd seen. The police needed to look for Dom and make sure he was all right.

He lifted himself from the floorboards and crawled slowly back to the ceiling panel that led to the ladder. When he'd positioned himself to lift the panel, he sat still and counted one hundred seconds again. Hearing no sounds from below, he steeled himself to leave his hiding place, then counted to one hundred yet another time. Leaving even this temporary safety was harder than he thought it would be.

He raised the tile and climbed slowly down, placing each foot carefully on the rung below, listening for any sound at all. When he reached the bottom, he peeked from behind the curtain and searched the empty auditorium for any signs of anyone else in the cavernous space.

He slid past the curtains, made his way down the left aisle to a door that led to the back stairs. He looked up the stairwell and listened, but heard only some remote background noises, sounds he was used to hearing in the building. He climbed the steps two at a time until he reached the fourth floor, then stopped to catch his breath.

Beyond the door was the hallway to Charles's office. He opened it slowly and peered around the corner.

Cindy's back was to him. She seemed focused on the computer screen, jotting notes on a legal pad.

He dusted his pants and straightened his shirt.

"Cindy." Parker approached her quickly.

She turned toward him, surprise on her face.

"Cindy, is Mr. Story in his office?" He hoped Charles was out. He didn't feel like talking to the lawyer for Mr. Smith right now.

"No. He's down the hall with some of the other partners."

"Cindy, listen to me." He leaned on her desk, his voice a hard whisper. "All hands on deck. There's a gunman in the building. First floor. You've got to call 911."

"What?" Her hazel eyes grew round.

"You have to call for help."

"I...I..."

"Now, Cindy. No time to waste." He stared into her eyes.

She flinched. "Yes, sure, I'll get Mr. Story right now."

"No—" he began.

"Wait in his office." She pointed to the door.

No.

"I'll be right back."

Well...

"I promise." Her eyes implored him to trust her.

"Yeah, yeah, okay." Parker turned, went into Charles's office and closed the door behind him.

CHAPTER 18

Dawson clenched his fists. Dealing with the university was the sheriff's job, not his, and they'd taken a bite out of his morning. He scanned the messages on his desk, prioritizing them, thinking about which could be handled by Rowe, which could wait for a couple of days, and which could be ignored.

He felt the day slipping away; the clock already reading nine-thirty in the morning. He pulled a pad from his desk and began a list of special items he'd need to search the area around the pump station: satellite phone, regular phone, reserve ammunition, and extra water. He wished the drone wasn't on the fritz.

Grace opened his door and barked, "Deputy Rowe on line two." She pulled her head back and closed the door before Dawson could reply.

He lifted the receiver. "Rowe, what's up?"

"You're not gonna believe this, but I'm in the hospital right now."

"What?"

"Yeah, I went to investigate the situation at the McCullum Ranch. Strange, I gotta say. Four sheep dead, all along an outcrop of rock on the western slope. Dead as doornails, lined up like they were gonna eat at a trough. Just laying out there in the pasture. No sign of what could've killed 'em."

"Strange, okay, but did you say at the hospital or in it?"

"Well, let me tell you...Bobby McCullum, the owner's son, was explaining how he rotates the sheep on the pasture, going over where they'd been the last few days, when we got back at the barn. He didn't know what to make of it, so we decided to call the vet to see if he had any ideas..."

"Yes?"

"Yeah, well, at the barn I was standing next to Mr. McCullum's Appaloosa mare, Molly. High spirited horse, you know. She was tied to the stall, but outside of it..."

"Rowe..."

"Well, I was writing in my pad and listening to Mr. McCullum when Molly stomped square on top of my left foot."

"What?"

"Yeah, I know, it was dumb, but I was distracted. I got too close and spooked her I guess 'cause next thing I knew I was in terrible pain, Dawson, just terrible."

He envisioned Rowe shaking her head. "Keep going."

"I about passed out, right there. Mr. McCullum caught me, laid me on the ground and called the ambulance."

Crap.

"So, I'm a little doped up right now but most of the pain is gone. They took x-rays and all. I'll be fine but a couple of those little bones in the foot have been fractured."

"Oh, man."

"Yeah, but I'll be okay. I just can't walk very far for a while. Doctor says he'll wrap my foot up good and send me home for some sleep. But I asked and he said I could go to work tomorrow or the next day, just I shouldn't put much weight on the foot for a couple of weeks. And they'll have to re-wrap it maybe every other day."

"I'm glad it wasn't anything more serious." Dawson rested his forehead in his hand. "So, when will we see you?"

"Tomorrow, hopefully. That's the plan. Man, my head is spinning, Dawson. I need to lay down again."

"Yes, do that Rowe, and don't worry about things here. I can get your ranch report later."

"Right. Thanks. Going now." She hung up.

Of all the things: a damn horse stomps on Rowe's foot. Dawson couldn't justify leaving the office today. And even if he could, he wouldn't reach the pump station until close to sunset. So, today, he would organize the work on his desk, give some work assignments to Grace, and try to leave tomorrow. Then he wondered about what had killed those sheep that way…

A disconnected thought occurred to him, and he dialed the intercom to talk to Grace.

"Hey, would you contact a student for me? Her name is Claire Lin, and she may have had a relationship with our deceased Professor Hollins. See if she will come in voluntarily for an interview with me today."

"Sure thing. Tomorrow okay if she can't today?"

"Not really. Well, if it's first thing in the morning…"

"On it."

"Thanks." He hung up.

If he could get to the pump station before noon tomorrow, he'd have a good stretch of time to search the area. He could even get back home after dark if he needed to.

The sheriff would return later in the week. Rowe's

foot injury wouldn't prevent her from driving or handling the in-office work until then. If Grace could go without him for half a day or so, he might be able to make some progress searching for the ponytail man. If he waited for the sheriff to return, he might lose the opportunity altogether.

Plan B would have to do.

CHAPTER 19

Where the hell was Cindy? Parker rubbed his palms against his thighs and glanced at the clock on Story's wall. Two minutes had felt like twenty. All he had were questions and there was a man with a gun in the building.

Finally, the door opened behind him, and although he was expecting it, indeed he was waiting for it, he jumped at the sound. Cindy hurried to the chair next to him. She moved it so they faced each other and handed him a bottle of water.

"It's all going to be okay, Parker," she said, leaning toward him.

"Oh?"

She placed her hands on his arm, nails painted a glossy pink. They seemed cold on his skin, but she smiled and nodded.

"The partners' meeting was over, but Mr. Story was still there, and I told him right away and he called building security. He also got you this water from the conference room kitchen and was on the phone with the police when I left to come back up here. The police will be here soon, and we'll all be all right."

"We have to warn people—"

"I told the other assistants. They're getting the word out."

"Oh, man, Cindy, what a relief." Parker's shoulders relaxed. The bottle of water had been opened, but it was full, so he twisted off the cap and took a long, luxurious, drink.

"What happened?" she asked, gently squeezing his arm.

He caught his breath and raised a finger, a sign to wait, while he swallowed another deep drink.

"Take your time" She slid her hands off his arm and clasped them together on her lap.

"Sure." He set the half-empty bottle on Charles's desk.

She smiled a perfect row of ivory teeth, and Parker's heartbeat seemed to flicker.

He told her about the blow-up between Dom and Betty, how he'd left Dom at his office and returned with his tools to find a man with a gun pointed at him. She cooed now and then as he spoke, a soft, mothering sound that kept him talking. He explained how he'd hidden above the rafters in the auditorium then made his way to her desk for help, the tale stealing a little of his breath.

She handed him the bottle of water again and he took another long drink.

"That's terrible," she said, but her eyes did not appear to share the sentiment. She stared at his face, watching dispassionately as his head seemed to fill with air, or helium, or something, rotating the room like a carousel.

"Hey," he began, then slumped into the chair and spun out of consciousness.

CHAPTER 20

Parker's head clunked against the ground and his eyes seemed to spin in their sockets. The scent of dust and sage filled his nostrils. He had a brief memory of being cold in the dead of night, but he'd been unable to move, unable to warm up. He heard himself groan.

"He's awake," a gruff voice declared.

"Get him up."

His torso lifted from the ground without volition, his feet sliding under his weight, knees buckling, then straightening and locking him upright. He glanced about, the motion sending a wave of dizziness through his brain.

Rough hands pulled the cell phone and housekeys from Parker's pocket. Another man took a phone and a set of keys from Dom.

For some reason, he couldn't move his hands from behind his back. The men herded Dom forward along the path. One of them turned and walked back to Parker, the front of his sweater coated in sand, hair tight against his head. His face seemed hollowed out somehow, his dark eyes sunk deep in their sockets—the man who'd pointed a gun at him back at the office.

Parker tried again to move his hands and realized they were tied together.

The man moved behind Parker and pulled upward on his arms, torquing his shoulders away from their sockets. Pain radiated through his back and neck and he yelped.

"Walk."

Parker stumbled forward.

"Follow them."

He tried to clear his head, shuffling one step at a time. They were on an open plain dotted with tufts of grass, sagebrush, and rock. The terrain rose and fell in gentle swells, a calm sea of solid ground. The other man walked ahead, shoulders stout, hair a boxy brown. Dom walked ahead of him, dried blood caked on the back of his head and neck.

He looked slowly from side to side. To his right and behind them lay the pumping station he and Dom had been to the day before. A big black pickup truck was parked a couple of yards from Dom's Bronco.

Blood pounded through his temples like a five-alarm hangover. Of course, he'd been drugged, but...

Cindy. Damn it. What was going on? Why were Betty and Cindy aligned? Had Cindy actually talked to Mr. Story? Where were these men taking them?

He looked to his left, where the land spread into the distance, fading into the horizon. The man behind him jabbed him in the back, a reminder of who was in charge.

They seemed to be following an old two-track, a route forged through the sagebrush by pickup trucks years ago. They descended a gentle slope and came into view of a wide canyon, a jagged knife-slice across the skin of the plateau. The dirt tracks faded away as the gorge deepened before them, sheer red cliffs on the other side of the crevasse.

The man ahead of him turned to his side and Parker could see he had a pistol. The man told Dom to stop.

"To the edge." The hollow-faced man poked Parker's back again. He moved to within a few feet of Dom and stopped.

Dom gave him a quick sideways glance; an assurance Parker thought was brave but empty.

"Turn around."

He and Dom turned to face the two men.

The gunman took two steps closer and raised a Glock-style pistol at Dom's forehead. He braced himself to fire.

CHAPTER 21

Relic moved to the back of the black pickup, out of sight from the men walking toward the steep canyon.

He had no idea why these four men were here, but it damn sure wasn't for anything good. He'd seen two of the men with guns wrestling and commanding the other two to walk ahead of them. One prisoner's hands were tied behind his back, the other's tied in front. The fact that they were heading to the gorge at gunpoint was a very bad sign.

For some reason, they'd driven two separate vehicles to the pump station—a shiny new truck and a pale, rusted-out Bronco, parked above the pumps and a few yards from each other. He didn't know what he was going to do next, but disabling the vehicles would at least put them on the same turf, literally. Boots to boots.

And the two who were being led to the cliff needed a hand, that much was certain.

He scurried across open ground to the Bronco and ducked by the driver's side. He opened the door and popped the lock on the engine compartment, then ran to the front and lifted the hood, searching for something to monkey wrench. The engine used the old points-and-distributor system, so he pulled the wire that ran from the distributor to the coil. The cylinders would not get a spark without it. The old Ford would be grounded.

Gently, he pushed the hood of the Bronco down until he heard the latch close. He could see the men about a half mile away, approaching the gorge.

Relic ran back to the pickup truck. They'd left the tailgate down after dragging one of the men onto the ground. Several cotton blankets lined the bottom and two silver plastic totes rested on the left side of the truck bed. He pulled one onto the tailgate and looked inside.

A gray toolbox anchored the bottom of the tote. A five-gallon container of gasoline was propped on one side. He lifted it easily—there was only about a half-gallon of fuel inside. Jumper cables and a tow rope were tangled together.

He reached for the other tote and opened it. A portable air pump, tire sealant, dirty rags, and a quart of oil had been tossed inside.

He stole a glance down the dirt road. The men

were nearly at the edge of the cliffs. If he was going to help them, he had to do it now.

Relic put the can of gasoline and the quart of oil on the ground. He moved to the side, uncapped the lid to the fuel tank on the truck, and stuffed a rag into the opening. He sprinkled gas onto the rag from the gasoline can and a little over the open bed of the truck. He poured oil onto one of the blankets.

He pulled matches from his pocket and lit the rag in the fuel tank, the flames taking quick hold of the cotton. He lit another match for the oil-soaked blanket on the bottom of the tailgate. In short order, it, too, had taken hold, black smoke billowing from the truck bed.

Relic ran toward the pumping station and dropped behind a desk-sized rock to watch. A column of smoke billowed from the pickup truck as he continued carefully toward the gorge, staying out of sight.

CHAPTER 22

"No, you idiot!" The hollow-faced man waved at the man with the Glock. "We shoot 'em only if we have to. We make this look like an accident." He pointed over the edge of the cliff, drawing Parker's gaze across the rocky gorge then back to their captors.

The man with the gun shook his head, the rebuke like a slap to his face.

"The cops will find 'em sooner or later." The hollow-faced man pulled him aside. "They find a bullet in their head, they know they were shot, right?"

The other man nodded.

"And if they ever find your gun, they match it to the bullet, right?"

"Right, Wicks."

"No names, bubba, remember?"

"Shit. Right." He stared at his feet, the pistol sagging by his side.

Dom rolled his eyes at Parker.

"What is this? Murder 101?" Dom's words bit into the air.

Parker could not appreciate the humor.

The hollow-faced man stepped closer, punching Dom hard in the stomach, driving his fist upward. Air rushed from Dom's lungs and he fell to his knees, his face suddenly purple, forehead creased in pain. His hands, still bound together with plastic zip ties, clutched at his chest.

"Hey…" Parker moved toward Dom, but the other man stepped directly in his path and pressed the barrel of the gun into the flesh above Parker's eyes. The man clamped his lips tightly together, ready to fire despite his partner's admonition.

"On your knees."

Parker had stopped, eyes on the blackened gun. Slowly, Parker moved backward and down, hating the power these men wielded over them.

Dom sucked short, desperate swallows of air.

Why would these men kill them? What the hell was going on?

The man moved away from Parker and pointed his gun in the air, a temporary de-escalation. The hollow-faced man patted him on the shoulder. "Now we toss 'em over."

Parker peered over the lip of the cliff again. The sharp ridge dropped precipitously, six hundred feet down to a jumble of massive boulders on the canyon floor. He gasped. His heel slipped closer to the edge, a fist-full of gravel pirouetting into the thin air, spinning outward, and he couldn't peel his eyes away until the first pebbles bounced against the rocks below, the disembodied sound echoing moments later, his foot just inches away from following them to the bottom.

Desperation rose in his chest, grasping upward, tightening his throat.

He leaned toward the ground, away from the high cliffs, and when he did, he saw something climbing into the air. "Hey," he heard himself croak, nodding toward the pump station.

The hollow-faced man tensed and turned to look behind him.

A column of storm clouds roped upward from the pickup truck, oily smoke swirling into the clear blue sky.

CHAPTER 23

"What the hell?" the hollow-faced man, the one called Wicks, stepped away from the others and pointed at Dom and Parker. "Stay with them," he commanded, running toward the truck.

The other man glared at each of them in turn.

"Don't blame me," Dom gasped, lifting his bound hands outward, his sense of humor intact.

"Me, either," Parker said, twisting to show his own hands, knowing it was a silly thing to say, but hoping it made the man snarl at him instead of Dom.

Whoosh!

They all turned to stare at the distant pickup truck, now fully ablaze; the fuel, tires, paint, all of it distorting the air with a tsunami of heat, bending the horizon into a mirage of undulating colors.

Wicks stopped about forty yards from the truck, staring at the scene.

Crack!

Parker could see the front windshield explode from expanding gas, the interior now flooded with air and flames and then the side windows split, mirrors popped, headlights fractured.

The hollow-faced man raised an arm to shield his eyes, but he stayed where he was, transfixed by the deadly fire.

Dom cleared his throat. He winked at Parker as he straightened, then took a deep breath.

What the hell are you doing, Dom?

Parker stayed still.

The gunman had lowered both arms to his side and was staring at the rising column of smoke.

Dom took a quiet step closer to him.

Parker shook his head, but Dom did not seem to notice.

The man shifted his weight from one leg to the other.

Dom leapt forward, arms outstretched like a hoop, slamming over the man's head, pinning his arms to his body.

The man squeezed a shot from the Glock, the bullet tearing into soil at his feet, the sound drowned by another explosion from the burning truck.

Dom had him now, his muscled arms squeezing the breath from the man, spinning him around to face the gaping gorge. The man's face turned crimson, eyes bulging, voice squeaking like a frightened mouse. The gunman struggled, first kicking his feet in the air then planting them onto the ground.

Dom seemed to lose thirty years of age; his hands zip-tied but gripping together too, a wrestler's determination to win.

Dom moved them ever closer to the edge and the man began to really panic, his pistol dropping to the ground, feet digging into the ground but slipping, slipping toward the edge.

Parker stood, unsure what he could do to help. He tested the ties on his hands, but they were unforgiving.

Suddenly, the man bent his knees, his feet found purchase against the bedrock, and they spun together, a full circle and a half. Dom's back was now to the cliff, the man shoving mindlessly, his voice still wheezing something desperate that Parker could not hear.

They took another step backward.

"Dom!" Parker stepped toward them.

The man flung his head back against Dom's and the two of them spun down to the ground together, landing hard against the rock, rolling toward the gorge and suddenly, without warning, they spun off the edge, into the empty air, and were gone.

CHAPTER 24

Claire Lin had agreed to see him at eight o'clock in the morning and, if she was prompt, Dawson could still get to Moonshine Mesa by mid-day and begin his search for the ponytail man.

He squeezed past Grace's station, her desk cluttered with papers, file folders, and two old phones, a table behind her stacked with radio equipment that had seen better days. A dusty dreamcatcher hung on the wall above the electronics. He left his office door open and plopped into the chair behind his desk. Bitter coffee in hand, he took a sip and stared at the ceiling, ill-defined thoughts roaming like ghosts.

At 8:07, Grace arrived with student Lin in tow. Grace knocked on the door frame and motioned for Lin to enter.

"Good morning, Ms. Lin." Dawson stood to greet her.

"Good morning," she said, shyness in her voice. She stood maybe five-feet-three-inches tall and might have weighed a hundred pounds wet.

"Please, have a seat." He pointed to the chair in front of his desk. "Can we get you some coffee?"

"No, thanks." She sat lightly in the chair and watched him expectantly.

"Probably a good choice," he said, making fun of the sheriff's coffee, but gaining not a smile or even a grimace in response. Her black hair was trim, her eyes and face an open, if bland, expression, but her fingers gave her away. She'd interlaced them in her lap and squeezed, her knuckles white. She was certainly nervous about something.

"Thanks for coming in," he sat back in his chair. "I'll get right to it. You know Professor Hollins died yesterday, right?"

Moisture filled her eyes. "Yes." She twisted her hands even tighter.

"Yes, so sorry to have to say it. We're questioning all the students at the archeologic site that day and you'd left early."

"Yes."

"Can you tell me why? You drove separately and left early, right?"

"Yes. I just started a new job at the Rathskeller, and they scheduled me that afternoon. I didn't want to make trouble. I knew it might affect my grade, but I'd explained it to Professor Hollins, and he said to work on the dig for as long as I could and not to worry too much about it."

Dawson chose his words carefully. "That was nice of him, huh?"

"Yes."

"Does he let all of his students participate in field work on such a…flexible schedule?"

She stared at her fingers, which were becoming a knotted mass. "I don't know about any other students…"

"Was your relationship with the professor anything special? Any reason he'd let you leave early like that?"

A tear dropped from her eyes onto her lap. "We were close for a while."

"I see."

Dawson let silence fill the room, hoping she'd continue.

"We were together for a while. Last year. But it ended, quickly." Her brown eyes rose to meet his, a silent plea for understanding.

"Last year?" he prompted.

"Yes, we knew it was against university rules,

but…" She shook her head. "Anyway, we broke it off after just a couple of months. I haven't been in a personal relationship with him since."

Dawson nodded.

"You don't have to report this to the college, do you?" Another plea in those wide eyes.

He waited a beat. "No. We don't care about that. We're just running down whatever information we can."

His words released the tension on her face, her hands finally pulling apart, her fingers flexing. She wiped her eyes. "I still like him, but not that way. He's a brilliant professor."

She'd given her confession. He was inclined to believe her about all of it. Besides, there was no way in hell that little Miss Lin could possibly have overpowered the bulky professor, let alone strangled him without signs of a struggle at the scene. Still, there was something else on her mind.

"What about anyone else?" he asked. "Any other students involved with him? Any professors? Anyone you can think of you might have had strong feelings about Hollins, one way or the other?"

She glanced at her lap. "Well, this is more in the nature of a rumor…"

"Yes?"

"Last fall, one of the guys on our dig…"

"…out at Cedar Flute?"

"…yes…he pocketed a really beautiful chert knife he'd found, antler handle and all."

"He stole it from the dig?"

"Well, that's the rumor. Professor Hollins found out and nearly got him expelled. He went before the Board of Regents and in a split vote they let him stay enrolled. He's on the dig this semester, too, and the professor was not happy about it. Maybe the student wasn't, either."

Dawson leaned forward. "One of the guys on the dig out there now?"

"Yes, if the rumor is true."

"Who?"

"I don't want to get in trouble for repeating a rumor…"

"This is a murder investigation, Ms. Lin. We'll keep your name out of it as much as we can, but we have to follow up any leads."

"Of course."

"Who is it?"

"I don't know him. I'm not sure of his last name, but his first name is William."

Will Cobb. One of the students first on the scene, the ones who had discovered Hollins's body. If Dawson remembered correctly, Will had checked Hollins's pulse after Keith Simmons had found the man. Dawson had all their names and contact information on his legal pad. This guy had just become a fresh lead.

He'd ask Deputy Rowe to interview Will Cobb tomorrow, after she was released from the hospital. She might be on crutches, but an interview wouldn't require much walking around.

He could still get himself out to the mesa this afternoon, back to his primary suspect—the ghost with a ponytail.

CHAPTER 25

Parker couldn't believe his eyes or his ears. Dom and the gunman were gone, fully out of sight, their grunting, furious struggle now deathly silent.

He moved carefully to the edge of the cliff and dared to look beyond.

There, hundreds of feet below, were two dark human forms, slapped haphazardly across the sandstone like wet clothes flattened out to dry.

A pocket of air burst from his lungs, a sob that floated across the deep canyon walls. It was all too sudden, too quick, too final for his mind to grasp. A nest of wasps loosened against his nerves, buzzing, prickling, stinging. He pulled back from the ridge.

Dom was dead.

A shift in the breeze brought the acrid smell of burning rubber to his nose and he turned to look. The truck was hardly recognizable anymore, just this blackened blob of smoldering oil and metal. The smoke had become a lighter shade of gray, its initial anger spent but with enough fuel to burn for hours.

The hollow-faced man continued to stare at the fire. He ran his hand over his scalp, an expression of dismay or frustration.

The scrape of boots on the ground made Parker spin to look behind him.

A man with a thin goatee and hair pulled tight against his head stepped toward him, palms raised, a sign that he came in peace. "Let me cut your hands free," he said.

"Who the hell are you? What are you doing here?"

"Name's Relic."

"Like a relic?"

"Sorry I couldn't help your friend," he nodded toward the cliff, "but there's time to help you." He moved closer. "Turn around, please."

"Hey!" The shout came from down the road. The man who'd been watching the truck was running toward them, pistol drawn.

Parker turned and held his hands out from his waist. He felt a tug, then an outward slice, and he was free. He rubbed his wrists, urging circulation back into his hands.

"Follow me." Relic spun, black ponytail bobbing against a large daypack.

The shooting pain Parker had felt earlier, the electric jolt against his nerves, had begun to deaden, some kind of mental narcotic pushing it away. He had no time to dwell on what had just happened with Dom.

He glanced at Wicks and watched him closing the distance between them.

Relic trotted along the cliff, away from the gunman, and Parker followed quickly. He reached a boulder the size of an overstuffed chair, perched at the lip of the gorge. He slid to the ground and scooted close to the edge of the cliff. A blue, multi-shaded climbing rope had been looped around the rock.

Relic pulled gloves from his hands and tossed them at Parker. "Put these on."

Parker put them on and stopped at the large stone.

"Follow me down." Relic slid his body over the rim and began lowering himself down the ropes.

Parker glanced behind him again. The gunman was closing quickly.

He crawled to the edge and peered over. Hell, no.

The ponytailed man had descended fifty feet already to a ledge that paralleled the rim of the canyon. Parker looked straight down the ragged gorge, suddenly lightheaded again. He tried to refocus on the ropes and wiggled his feet over the edge of the cliff.

He could hear the gunman's footfalls. Now was not the time for a fear of heights.

Here goes nothing.

The gloves were well-worn leather and helped him keep a good grip. One rope had gone over the boulder, around it, then back down the cliff so the rope was doubled on the way down.

Now, he could see the gunman gaining ground, so he slipped as quickly as he could farther over the rim, his weight pulling his arms straight, his shoes swinging into empty space. He hurried, hand over hand, down the ropes until the plateau disappeared above him. Rough rock scraped against his chest as he went, but he kept a steady pace, trying not to panic.

He didn't know where this guy Relic was taking him, but he guessed it didn't really matter, so long as it was away from Wicks and the place where Dom and the other gunman had gone over the edge.

He felt a hand guide his foot to a solid spot in the wall, the ledge he'd seen earlier. "Let go of the rope."

Parker did as he was told and grabbed a lip of stone at eye level. Relic pulled one of the ropes downward, working quickly, wrapping it into a loop. The other end of the rope wiggled up the cliff toward the anchored rock, then around and past it, falling loosely toward them. Relic continued to wind the rope onto itself then scurried down the ledge.

The gunman stuck his head over the edge and shouted obscenities at them.

Parker grinned, just a little, at the man's frustration.

Then the hollow-faced man reached outward, pointing his pistol down the side and the cliff and right at Parker's head.

CHAPTER 26

Boom!

Relic had him by his shirt and wrenched him violently to his right, nearly twisting him off the ledge. His left shoulder went suddenly numb, his arm flopping loose by his side, his strength dissolved. He put his right hand in the stranger's, and Relic yanked him along the uneven rock.

Heat rose in Parker's cheeks, adrenaline and anger boiled upward as he realized the gunman had shot him.

Relic hurried them along the narrow path, Parker stumbling over loose stones, Relic tugging him farther and farther along in a race to safety.

Boom!

Parker glanced upward but could no longer see the hollow-faced man.

"Look at me!" Relic yelled, his grip tightening on Parker's fingers until they hurt even through the glove.

The ledge dipped abruptly downward. Parker's shoes slipped and slipped again, stones rolling him forward like a set of ball-bearings, but Relic kept the pressure on Parker's right hand, pulling him at a reckless pace.

Relic slowed for a moment then jerked Parker's arm again, the pain jabbing his neck. They slid to another level spot and the ledge opened up, widening to nearly two feet. Relic increased their pace as the path dropped more steeply.

"Hey…" Parker wanted to slow down.

"Look at me," Relic said again, pointing to his own eyes then glancing ahead, leading them along the easiest route.

"Slow down," Parker barked, but the man's ponytail bobbed against his pack as they shuffled forward, stepping over stones, working their feet to keep their grip along the sandstone rim. Parker had to focus on the placement of his feet.

Surely, they were beyond the reach of the gunman now, but Relic tugged at him with steady determination, bringing them down, down, into the gut of the toothy canyon. Their path curved left against the face of the cliff and they angled across the shelf, skidding quickly over loose gravel. Parker lost his balance for a moment, dropping to his knees, but Relic held tight to his hand and propelled them onward.

They reached another curve in the cliff and the rim tapered to a scant few inches.

Parker felt wetness on his shoulder. He turned to look, and Relic yelled at him again. "Eyes ahead. Hold on."

Parker watched the sheer wall where Relic was leading them, and his heart pumped faster. Relic ran his right palm against the bluff, fingers searching for dents and knobs on the stony face, tiny holds in the vertical rock. He refreshed his grip on Parker's hand and led them slowly now, jamming the toes of his boots against the wall with each small step.

Parker could see the muscles on Relic's right arm straining to stabilize their trek, his hand sliding to a new crag in the rock, feet pulling them along, then doing it again and again in micro-steps. Parker leaned into the rough sandstone, shuffling to match Relic's moves, his left arm still limp and useless.

Relic's daypack clung tightly against his shoulders, silhouetted against the blue sky. Parker's eyes followed the arc of the pack down the precipice, and the sudden drop buoyed his gut and twisted his eyes in their sockets.

CHAPTER 27

Wicks stared down into the gorge, surprised that Parker had gotten away, puzzled by the sudden appearance of another man to help him. They were beyond his reach now. Whoever had helped Parker get away must have torched the truck as a distraction.

He stood and moved northeast, to the spot where his associate and Dom had wrestled each other over the edge. A Glock 17 lay on the ground, so Wicks picked it up and tucked it under his belt. He crawled to the edge and looked over.

Both men were just tiny figures below, but their backs twisted severely out of place, arms and legs splayed against the rocks.

He stood and turned back to the smoking truck. He dusted off his pants and walked to the burning mess, the smoke beginning to thin. Sunlight filtered through the toxic fumes, casting an eerie glow on the truck, the

Bronco, and the trailer house.

He'd driven Dom's Bronco to the pump station, following the truck that now smoldered on the road. He'd left the keys in the ignition. He climbed in and turned over the engine, again and again, but the damned rust bucket wouldn't start. It had run just fine on the way here.

Damn it to hell. Whoever had helped Parker and Dom must have messed with the Bronco, too.

He walked to the old house trailer, pulled the cell phone from his pocket, and dialed. He explained the situation to Mr. Smith, who cursed a streak that would make a prison inmate blush.

When Smith seemed to run out of steam, Wicks said, "Boss, I need some help, but I need someone with experience in these…situations."

Smith grunted.

"I'm not blaming my partner. I'm just saying…"

"Yeah," Smith barked. "I get it. My best guys are on another job. You're way in the middle of nowhere. They can't get to you today. I'd say, midday tomorrow at best."

"I won't sit on my ass. I'll get into the canyon and try to track them down. But they might circle back."

"Keep me informed, Wicks."

"Sure, but…I'll probably be in and out of cell phone service here."

Smith grunted again.

"But I'll follow them and let you know as soon as I can."

"Right." Smith hung up.

Sometime tomorrow, more men would arrive to help. They would bring fresh weapons and supplies. At least two of them could use the trailer as a command center and scour the plateau. Wicks would find a way down the gorge from farther east, where the canyon began as a shallow arroyo, and chase the two who'd gotten away.

They were going to find these little assholes and finish the job.

CHAPTER 28

"Stay on me," Relic spoke each word clearly, but Parker could not peel his eyes away from the void below.

"Hey, hey!" Relic yelled, crushing Parker's hand in his grip, the pain of it slowly tugging his focus upward, back to the leathered face of the man on the ledge beside him.

"We're almost there." Relic turned his head away.

Parker tried to banish his fear, focusing on the texture of the rock in front of his nose and on each moment as it led to the next and the next. Each breath, one at a time. He leaned tighter into the face of the cliff, scraping his way along. They advanced an inch or two with each move and, though part of him knew it was not that long, the journey seemed to stretch into hours.

The shallow ledge widened unexpectedly, and Relic pulled him faster down the shelf. They no longer hugged the bluff but instead began a series of switchbacks to a level area about fifty feet above the canyon floor. A rim of rock sheltered the space like a sombrero. Grass and cacti had rooted into the ground, spaced apart by the dry desert conditions.

Relic kept his hand on Parker's and led them to a shaded spot at the base of the sandstone, an older brother leading a little kid. He motioned for Parker to sit.

Parker finally looked at his left shoulder, his shirt soaked with blood.

My god. He realized again that he'd been shot.

His knees softened like deflated tires, barely able to guide his descent to the ground. He leaned into his right side, keeping the injured shoulder away from the dirt, and struggled to sit up.

Relic had removed his pack and was searching through it. "What's your name?"

Parker began to unbutton his shirt. "Parker."

"Why are those men after you?" Relic brought a bandage, a flask, and a water bottle from his pack.

"Hell if I know." The smell of his own blood made his stomach curl. He peeled the cloth from his shoulder, the sucking sound like an orange peel being separated from its fruit. He felt lightheaded.

Relic pushed him gently to a more comfortable position and leaned his back against the cliff. He removed the lid from the bottle of water and slowly poured it over the wound. Parker winced. They could see a gash across the top of his shoulder, but the bullet seemed to have missed anything vital.

Relic set the water on the ground and opened the flask. "Take a swig." He handed it to Parker. The sting of moonshine cleared his nostrils and he took a quick, greedy drink. The liquor was stronger than he'd expected, and he coughed.

Relic took back the flask. "Hold tight." He poured a trickle of it over the wound and Parker cursed, writhing under the sharp pain, taking his breath in short gasps.

"Again." Relic dribbled it over the gash, and it hurt like hell but not as badly as the first time; thankfully, he did not pour it again. Instead, Relic squeezed ointment from a tube onto the raw slice and wrapped a clean bandage over the wound, under Parker's arm, over and under again, and tied it off over the top.

When Relic was done, Parker took a long, deep breath, and stretched his legs out in front of him. Relic handed him the flask again, so he took another good swig, relishing the warmth as it spread through his stomach. His shoulder was sore, but his other muscles relaxed a little and he turned onto the ground on his right side.

Shadows followed the sun as it arched across their

little shelter. Relic wore a thin, button-up shirt the color of red dirt and cargo pants with holes at the edges of the pockets. Scuffed and beaten, his boots must have endured an avalanche of rocks, a hundred thousand miles on exhausted soles. A thin goatee hung from his chin like shredded ribbons, shifting in the breeze, some sort of desert sasquatch.

Parker had a hundred questions, but exhaustion quickly won out, pulling him into a deep, mid-morning, snooze.

CHAPTER 29

Dawson stopped for a moment on a rise in the road above the pump station, watching the seared husk of a pickup truck. Several yards from that sat a rusted Bronco and, behind that, the old trailer house.

Someone was here.

He radioed the office, reporting where he was and what he'd found. Grace told him she'd heard from rancher McCullum, who'd said the veterinarian had decided his sheep had died of nematode parasites in their digestive systems. McCullum needed to do a better job of de-worming his herd.

Grace warned him to wait for back-up, and Dawson asked just who that would possibly be on this fine morning in the middle of the outback, Sheriff Leavitt out of town, Deputy Rowe with an injured foot. She didn't argue the point and they signed off the call.

He coasted a little closer then stopped and checked

his gear. He exited the county Jeep and walked to the pickup truck. He kept a suspicious eye on the trailer house, checking for signs of habitation. A man could hide among the electric pumps, too, rows of humming units the size of stout RV's and pipes running into and out of the earth.

The front grill was hot and though the cab had twisted somewhat in the heat, the frame was intact. The license plates were melted beyond recognition, glass shattered over the ground.

At least he didn't find any bodies.

He walked to the Bronco and circled it, inspecting it for signs of fresh damage or other evidence. He noticed a set of keys in the ignition and jotted the license plate number on his notepad.

Dawson returned to his Jeep and contacted Grace again, reporting more detail and asking her to check the license plate and also for contact information about the pump station itself. He waited a few minutes, watching the pumps and trailer house for any sign of movement or recent activity.

Grace radioed back that the Bronco belonged to Dominic Ubaldi, age 68, an employee of Sapphire Solutions. He asked her to try to track down Dominic—see if she could contact the man. She confirmed that the pump station was on federal land but hadn't found out yet who held the lease.

She warned him that although the trailer seemed to be within range of a cell tower, a park service report said that phone coverage away from the pumps would be spotty or non-existent.

She also said a ranch hand, some thirty miles away, reported seeing black smoke from the area, so the fire was fresh, something he knew already from the lingering heat of the truck.

"Want me to notify the feds?" she asked him.

He grunted his distaste.

"I know, but you're on land that's under a federal lease now," she said.

"The professor's death occurred in our jurisdiction, just outside the park."

"It's up to you, boss…" her voice trailed away.

"Remember how they treated us in the Devil's Tail case?"

"I do—"

"—those jackasses." They'd beaten the sheriff to the press, taken all the credit for solving an old diamond heist case and saving a group of river rafters. Dawson got a quick mention at the end of the story as someone the feds had "consulted." Consulted! "Hell, they had no clue about any of it until after we'd saved the lives of those campers."

"I know," she said softly.

"Right now, it just looks like vandalism here. I don't see any connection to anything serious, except that our mystery witness with a ponytail came up on the mesa and this would be a good place to leave a car for a getaway. Maybe he's this Dominic Ubaldi guy. Or a friend of his."

"Right."

"So, if I'm out of phone range for a while, it's because I'm searching the area and it could take all day, maybe some of tomorrow, so don't go calling the sheriff or the park service or anyone else for a while, all right?"

"Yes, deputy."

He nodded in satisfaction. "Signing off…"

Why had Dominic Ubaldi come out to these pumps? Or had someone else taken his vehicle?

Dawson locked the Jeep and returned to the truck. He pulled his pistol from the holster and moved carefully toward and around the trailer house. It seemed to be deserted. He tried the front and rear doors. Both were locked.

"Weird," he said to himself.

He holstered his weapon and noticed fresh tracks

leading from the trailer to the burned-out truck, then along a pathway to the west, toward a deep gorge that scarred the plateau. Dawson followed the tracks, stopping frequently to look about. He eventually reached the edge of the cliffs and noticed a scurry of boot prints in the dust near the rim. He knelt to examine the marks, placing a finger in one of the depressions.

"Fight," he said. "There was a fight here, and…" he followed a set of chevrons to the very edge of the cliff, lowered himself to the ground, and crawled until his head stretched over the rim.

Two bodies, maybe six hundred feet below, lay flattened against the bottom of the gorge.

"Damn." He pushed away from the edge. "Damn it."

He stood and glanced back the way he'd come, back toward the burned-out pickup truck and, just as he placed one foot forward, the ground beside him leapt into the air, and he knew what it was even before the sound reached his ears. He spun back toward the cliff, running along the rim as another patch of earth spit next to him, another gunshot aimed low and to his left. His boots pounded the ground. His mind raced, knowing each stride could be his last, each clomp of his boots, each step terrifyingly slow, clomp, clomp, clomp, until he reached a boulder and threw himself to the ground, scrambling behind it, waiting for another shot.

CHAPTER 30

Bright afternoon sun and an ache in his shoulder made Parker open his eyes. A small ring of rocks had been stacked several feet from his face, firewood laid next to that. He felt a weight on his body and, when he shifted, he found a fleece jacket spread over his legs and a rain poncho tucked around his torso.

He looked for the ponytailed man who called himself Relic, but he did not see him.

His skin felt stiff as a mummy's, his muscles pained and rigid. It took him three tries to prop himself on his elbow and finally sit up. A chill made him pull the poncho around him, his arms tucked inside.

A large daypack rested on the back of their rock shelter. An insulated mug marked "Holiday Expeditions" rested outside the fire ring.

Boots scraped across the sandstone floor and the man with the ponytail filled his view, imposing and stern.

He knelt near the fire ring, saying not a word. Dark eyes watched Parker closely, penetrating as searchlights, crow's feet like fissures in granite.

Parker waited for the man to speak but instead he offered his flask.

"Yes, thank you." Parker slid his arms from under the poncho and took the moonshine.

"No worries," Relic mumbled, but Parker wasn't sure whether the man really meant it.

Parker rubbed his eyes then took a careful sip. Sharp, a little like gin, and welcome.

"Thank you. For helping me." Parker peered over the top of the container.

"Sure. Sorry I couldn't help the man who was with you."

"I'm…" his words disappeared like smoke. The image of Dom lying at the bottom of the canyon rose like a demon and thickened his tongue. He coughed a short sob, hiding behind the flask.

Relic sat by his pack, cross-legged. "He was your friend."

The words were spoken without remorse, without the wail of emotion, but with reverence.

"Yes." Parker took a swallow, letting the heat of it burn down his throat.

Anger rose, sadness dropped, and guilt enveloped him, all of it a foaming surf churning against his chest.

"What brings you out to the desert?" Relic wound a cloth dressing around his hand and pulled a wicked looking blade from its sheath. He cut a length of the dressing with a practiced slice and tucked it back into his pack.

Parker tried to focus on the here and now. "I work for a place in Grand Junction, across the state line. It's kind of a property management company, owned by a big law firm there." Parker took another long sip, feeling the gin take greater effect.

Relic returned his knife to its sheath.

Parker felt his forehead begin to sweat.

"You okay?" Relic asked.

"Cold earlier…a little hot right now." He slid the poncho off his shoulders.

"We'll clean and wrap that wound again tomorrow."

"Tomorrow?"

"You're feverish and you've just had a couple shots of gin. Any more hiking now will get you a heat stroke. Probably in less than a mile." Relic looked him in the eye. "You want that?"

"No, of course not." He waited a beat. "Hey. Thanks."

"No worries." Despite his gruff manner, Relic

seemed to mean it. "You want to tell me why that guy was shooting at you?"

"I wish I knew."

"You must know something about it." Relic rearranged several items in his pack. "What brought you out to that oil field? Something to do with your job?"

"Yeah. Dom—that's the man who…" His windpipe drew tight again. "Dom and I work together. Worked together. Good guy. He was getting ready to retire…" the words fluttered in his chest, wrens swirling in place.

Relic gave him a moment.

"Dom was showing me the ropes. Anyway…" he cleared his throat. "Our boss, Betty Coulter, asked us to replace the pressure gauges at an old oil pump station, the one above us." He nodded his chin upward. "She runs a tight ship, but when we got there, we noticed the gauges were messed up. They'd been pre-set or something. They were stuck on a pressure reading—a psi—that was different from what the ones on the pumps were reading. We checked, and all the new ones seemed broken. Dom said they were 'crooked,' like someone wanted them to read a certain psi. We went back home that night and the next day…" he stopped.

Relic handed him a water bottle and he took a long, deep drink.

"Dom and I went to Betty's office to ask her about it. Dom was pretty pissed off. He wanted a confrontation, I could tell." He looked up at Relic. "I didn't want to make waves, but he didn't trust Betty. Anyway, he found a report in her desk marked confidential and we found out that Betty is the chief financial officer for a company that holds, that controls, the pump station."

"The company you work for?"

"No, another one, I think. Solar Gem or something like that."

Relic returned the water to his pack.

"Dom said a huge grant of money was to be transferred to the company that Betty's part of and it was to be paid," he thought for a moment, "in the next day or so. Then Betty showed up and the fireworks started. She tried to fire Dom, but he quit. I didn't know what to do, but I didn't want to rock the boat, so I followed him back to his office. He was getting his personal stuff to take home. He wasn't going to come back to work there—he was quitting right then and there. He had me get some of his personal tools and when I got back, Dom was gone. But then a man with a gun was in his office. He pointed it right at me." Parker pointed his finger out across the open canyon, thumb raised like the hammer on a six-shooter.

"Shit on a shingle." Relic leaned forward.

"Yeah. It was the same guy who shot at us as we were climbing down the cliffs." Parker tried to clear his head. "Anyway, I ran and I hid in the rafters above the auditorium in the building. When I was pretty sure the man was gone, I climbed down and went to tell Cindy, Mr. Story's assistant. He's a partner in the law firm that owns Sapphire Solutions. Indirectly, we all work for him and his firm. Cindy went to find him and call for help. She came back with water for me, and I drank it and started telling her what was going on. We were waiting for Mr. Story to get back when I just…I got dizzy and blacked out, I guess."

"Something in the water?" Relic raised a brow.

"Yeah." Parker let the truth of it sink in. "Next thing I know, I'm at the pump station again, hands tied up. So is Dom. These two guys march us to the edge of the cliff."

"Sounds like a cluster," Relic said.

"It's enough to…" Parker's words faded away.

"Make you dot your tees and cross your eyes?"

"Yeah…"

"So, Cindy, Charles Story, and Betty are working together, along with those two goons." Relic counted each name on his fingers.

Parker released a deep sigh. "She was so pretty."

"Who?"

"Cindy."

"Can't judge a book by its cover."

"I know, I know." He was done pining for Charles's assistant.

"They took you and Dom to the cliff. I saw them drive up. When I saw the two of you tied up, I knew you were in trouble."

"You were just up there on a hike or something?" Parker asked.

"Or something." Relic nodded, leaving it there.

"Do you live around here?"

"Yeah."

"And you torched the truck?" Parker asked.

"Yep. I thought a distraction might loosen up some possibilities."

"Then you came back to the cliff?"

"Yep. I saw Dom put one of the gunmen in a bear hug, then, sorry to say, both of them went over the cliff. His hands were tied together, so once he had his arms down around the gunman, I think he couldn't just…let go."

"Yes." Parker's chin fell to his chest.

"He saved you."

"So did you."

Relic thought for a moment. "Were the old pressure gauges reading higher or lower than what the new gauges were reading?"

"What? Higher, I guess."

"So, they didn't like the low psi readings." Relic tugged on his goatee.

"Why would that matter?" Parker rested his forehead in his hand.

CHAPTER 31

Dawson hid behind a low rock, trying to steady his hands, breathing in through his nose, out through his mouth, in, out, slowing his heart rate. The air had become deathly quiet.

The gunman had taken him by surprise, a mistake that could have quickly ended his life. He cursed himself for underestimating the risks.

He rested his head against the bare sandstone, smelling the dust of it, gathering his thoughts. He peeked quickly over the edge, scanning for signs of the shooter. The gunshot had sounded like a pistol, maybe a Glock, so the gunman had no special advantage over him in that respect. But whatever was happening at the pump station was no mere vandalism.

He lifted his head higher and continued to search for any sign of the man, to no avail. An unusual warmth spread across his right thigh and when he bent to check, he could see his own blood soaking his pant leg.

Damn it. He'd been hit. He flexed his knee and it seemed alright. But he didn't like the amount of blood on his leg. He knew that some measure of shock was keeping the injury from being painful, and he also knew that the natural anesthesia would pass. When that happened, it was likely to hurt like hell.

He scanned the area again. If the man was hiding, he was either lying down in the grass somewhere or back behind the burned-out truck, maybe thirty or forty yards away. Out of range for an accurate pistol shot. He hoped.

It was time to get up and move.

He scooted his legs underneath him and rose above the rock.

No one tried to shoot at him. He still couldn't see the gunman, but of course he was out there, somewhere between Dawson and his Jeep.

He was going to have to move away from the pumps and the vehicles, out across the rolling plateau. He put his full weight onto the injured leg, and it stung but it held, so he began walking sideways, watching the distant truck, hand on his pistol. After several steps, he turned and hurried over a low rise and out of sight of the station and truck.

Dawson had never been on Moonshine Mesa,

but he knew from the maps that moving south and east would take him to the cliffs above the Cedar Flute ruins. Maybe there was a way down to them and to the dirt road back to town. His radio was back in his Jeep. His phone would be beyond the reach of any cell tower for several miles, even at the ruins. He had one water bottle and a couple of protein bars. He could walk for miles, losing himself in this country, avoiding the gunman. But he'd need water soon, and if he lost much more blood, the gunman may have done his job after all.

Dawson stopped looking behind him. Either he was well ahead of the gunman or the man had stopped following him. As long as he wasn't shooting at him, he didn't care anymore. He was tired of searching for him.

He glanced at his wet pant leg. The bullet must have clipped him just above the knee. He wanted to find someplace to rest.

The desert sun lifted steadily into the sky as he walked to the west, toward the edge of the cliffs that led down to the ruins. Those cliffs were still miles away, though, and his water bottle was only partly full. He wound his way around another rise in the ground, shuffling between dry sage brush and ankle-high grass. The plateau lifted gently against the horizon and he hiked on and on until it dropped a few feet, the trough of an earthen wave. To his left stood a small hill of rock and he headed in that direction, hoping there was shade.

Something caught his eye and he twisted to look. Nothing but sage and a few scattered cedars toward the horizon. Bumps in the ground collected against the roots of native bunch grass, fist-sized anchors against erosion. No movement anywhere, except the sway of the grass.

He continued toward the small hill and discovered a shallow cave the size of a closet, partly hidden below the surface. He scrambled into the sandy bottom and sat near the center, out of the sun.

He took a short drink of water and examined his leg. He couldn't tell how deeply the bullet had scored, and the bleeding was not heavy. Still, the blood seemed to seep at a steady pace. He wished again that he had his bug-out bag with him, complete with energy drinks, ready to eat meals, water filter, first aid kit, and more. All of it in the back of his Jeep.

Dawson knew he had to get back to the pump station and his radio. He'd told Grace to ignore him for a while, an order that, in hindsight, was a mistake. The man with the pistol was still out there, searching for him or maybe holed up at the old trailer house. He resolved to go no farther across the plateau but instead to circle back and try to surprise the man. For now, he'd stay out of the heat. Evening could be a good time to return to the scene, anyway, with the sun at his back, glaring in the eyes of anyone looking for him.

He cut his pants away near the wound, just enough to get at it. He removed his outer shirt and T-shirt, then tied the T-shirt around his thigh. He put his uniform shirt back on and lay back, listening for any unusual sounds.

He must have dozed for a moment because a low snap woke him abruptly. He undid the strap on his holster, pulled his Glock, and laid it on his lap.

It could be anything, he thought. A snake. A hawk. A ground squirrel, most likely.

Or it could be the gunman, stalking him.

He shifted his feet beneath him, ready to move if he had to, and peered around the sheltering rocks.

Nothing.

Then, he heard something again, the other direction, a tiny sound, the break of dry grass maybe.

CHAPTER 32

Parker woke quickly, the pain in his shoulder rousing him. The afternoon had slipped past, blending into night. A faint moonglow spread dim shadows outside their little shelter. Relic leaned close to the wood and lit a small fire, blowing gently on the twigs. When it caught, the flames cast a wide, undulating glow across their little camp.

Relic ran his fingers through his goatee, a caveman grooming for the evening. "You feelin' okay?" he asked.

"Worn down. Lightheaded too."

"You've likely had a fever. That bullet wound was a real shock, and you lost some blood, and now you're fighting off an infection."

"Great," Parker mumbled.

"Drink some of this." Relic handed him the water.

"I'm hungry but I don't feel like eating. Does that make sense?"

"Yep. Here, you need some calories." He handed

Parker a bag of peanut M&M's, the misshapen orbs partially melted and clumped together. Parker put a handful into his mouth, the sweetness overwhelming. He chewed and washed it down with water then reached for the flask of gin. They sat quietly for a while, Parker taking several good sips of the liquor, thinking he should stop. But each swallow slid down more smoothly than the last.

Gently, Relic took the flask and put it back into his pack.

"Don't want me to keel over, is that it?" Parker nodded at the flask.

"Keel over. Are you a sailor? Do you live by the ocean?"

"No. I live in Colorado."

"You use a lot of nautical expressions for a land lubber," he grinned.

"I do?"

"Keel over, rock the boat, make waves."

"I guess I do sometimes…"

"It's all good. A lot of things are so ingrained in us, we don't even realize it."

"You know, I'm not even sure where 'keel over' comes from," Parker said.

"Keel over—like the keel of a boat is upside down."

"Oh. I just meant that I'd fall over."

"When a boat falls sideways, it's keeled over. In trouble."

"Oh, right. I don't want to keel over."

"I want you to be ship shape." Relic's teeth gleamed in the firelight.

"A little gin can help with that." Parker flexed his aching shoulder.

"You're a grown man." Relic handed the flask back to him.

"Right." He took another long swallow.

"What else do you know about what's going on?" Relic asked.

"Oh!" Parker straightened his back. "Yes." He pulled papers from his back pocket and unfolded them. He counted three pages, each with "confidential and privileged" stamped on the bottom. He studied them carefully.

"These are the pages Dom took from Betty's report. She's the CFO of the holding company that manages the pump station. Like I said before, the holding company is owned by Sapphire Solutions, the company the law firm owns."

"Sounds like a shit show," Relic grumbled.

Parker took another swig. "There's a group called Global Green Engineering. They've approved a grant of…"

Relic tilted his head as if to say: "What else?"

"Fifty-five million shollars." The gin was getting to him. "I mean dollars."

"Shit."

"All to the holding company Betty is part of. And," he flipped to another page, "get this—Charles Story owns the holding company Sholar Gem. So-ler Gem," he corrected himself.

Relic shook his head. "Why a holding company?"

"It's probably to keep his ownership a secret from the law firm. And everyone else." Parker rubbed his forehead. "But the fifty-five million is to expand the pump station. What's wrong with that?" He took another quick drink.

"There's something wrong with the station," Relic said. "Remember, the pressure is lower than it should be, and they want to hide that fact."

"But the engineering company, Global Green, would find out about it, eventually. Wouldn't they?"

"Maybe. Maybe not."

"Or," Parker wiped his forehead again, a low-grade heat unmooring his thoughts. "They only need to hide it for a little while."

"They've got something else planned here,"

Relic said.

They sat in silence for a minute.

Relic stared at Parker, a question in his eyes. "Got something specific on your mind?"

"Well..." Why not tell the man? Parker thought. He's a recluse—who's he going to tell? "Yeah."

Relic waited for more.

"I met a big shot client of Charles's called Mr. Smith. Well, it turns out that Smith shells...sells...drugs. Fen...fentanyl and more." He stared into the waves of fire. "My sister took the same kinda pills, the same damn pills, pink and blue like candy, and she went to sleep."

Relic watched him.

"Yeah. She never woke up."

"Oh, man. I'm so sorry."

Parker nodded. "Yeah. And Charles Story got Smith off, schott-free."

"Oh, man."

"Yeah." Parker closed his eyes. His head seemed to spin on an axis and he laid back onto the ground and slid into a restless sleep.

CHAPTER 33

Betty glanced at her Manager of the Year award that hung on the wall and smiled. She touched up her lipstick and checked her mascara, then tucked her mirror into her purse and walked purposefully to the elevator. She turned to start down the hall to Charles's office and heard him and Cindy, murmuring near her computer screen.

"Yes, those will do just fine," he told Cindy.

"Are you sure? We could get better seats for just a little more."

"That's true. Maybe go ahead, if you can get them."

Betty slowed her gait, listening in.

Cindy glanced up, her eyes two pale saucers. She touched Charles's arm.

He turned and hesitated for a second. "Betty! Glad to see you. Cindy's helping me get tickets to that country concert next month." He straightened.

"Charles, I need you for a few minutes." Betty

pointed toward his doorway.

"Of course." He turned and led her into his office.

Betty closed the door behind her. "Country music?"

"I promised my niece, Katy." He walked behind his desk and sat. "She's fourteen next month and dying to go."

"We'll be gone next month…" she whispered.

"Yes, yes, we will, but no one must think so. We've got to keep on with our lives as if we'll be here, right?" His voice was low.

"Uh…"

"We've got to keep up appearances…" His hands opened an invisible book, his silver-blue eyes beseeching her to agree.

"I suppose so. But we leave in three days."

"All the more reason to stay calm about it. We're almost there, Betty. Almost there."

"That's what we need to talk about." She sat in the chair across from his desk, mindful of the distance and authority it represented to his clients. And to her, for just a few days more. "The problem with the pressure readings…?" she began.

"Yes?"

"I sent Dom and the new guy, Parker, out to the site to replace the gauges. As you suggested, Mr. Smith got us a whole new set with the readings frozen, that's the word he used, frozen at the psi we need to satisfy Global Green."

"Right."

"Well, Dom went out there and figured out that the new ones were all stuck on the higher readings. Dom decided the new ones were broken so they kept the old ones in place and came back with the new ones."

Charles shook his head.

"But that's not all." She leaned forward. "Dom went to my office with the new gauges and started going through stuff on my desk." She took a breath. "He found the confidential report on the holding company and the funding we expect from Global Green in the next couple of days."

"He can't understand that report, Betty. He can't possibly figure out what that means."

"No, no, Charles. He did figure out part of it. He knows we've been tampering with the pressure readings and that Global Green Engineering is transferring their funding to us this week. And I think he knows I'm the chief financial officer of Solar Gem." She felt the blood rushing to her cheeks.

"What the hell was he doing in your desk?"

"He's a snoop. He's a piss ant little man who sees

conspiracies wherever he looks," she sneered.

"He's also retired his way out of here. When is it?"

"A couple more months, but I fired his ass right then and there."

"You did?"

"I threw him out of my office and told him to be out of the building immediately."

"Has he left?"

She clasped her hands together. "Yes. And Charles…"

"Yes?"

"When I flipped through the report, I found a couple of pages missing."

"You think he took them?"

"Why else would they be missing? So, I don't know if I overreacted or not, but I couldn't find you and Dom's become a loose cannon, and I got really worried, so I called Mr. Smith for help."

"Be-tty…" He drew out her name, raising it an octave, a scolding tone.

"Don't worry. Mr. Smith will take care of it. I told him we needed Dom and Parker to disappear, just for a few days, until Global Green makes the money transfer." She watched Charles's lips tighten, his eyes shifting from one side to the other. She knew him well enough to guess what he was thinking but would never say out loud—that Smith's men might kill Dom and Parker and though he hadn't planned on anything like that, no he didn't like that part, he also thought that Betty had done the right thing, what had to be done. He wanted to find a flaw in her decision to call Mr. Smith, but he couldn't.

"What about the pressure readings on the gauges?" he asked.

Betty's smile blossomed with self-satisfaction. "Smith's guys will remove the working gauges and install the pre-set ones when they are out there. Global Green will see the readings we want them to see."

Charles rubbed his forehead, eyes darting across his desk, chewing his lower lip. When he seemed to settle on an idea, he looked at her again. "Okay. Smith is in contact with you?"

"Yes."

"The whole building will know pretty soon that Dom's been fired. So be ready to explain that you caught him with attorney-client files or such. Parker, too. Tell people you're looking for replacements this week, something like that. That will explain their disappearance."

"Yes, of course." She rested her fingers on the edge of his desk. "We're still all set, though, right?"

"Of course," he relaxed his shoulders. "In three

days, we'll be out of here forever."

She released a sigh. "I'm all packed, Charles, and I'm feeling a little high-strung right now. It's hard to be patient..." They would fly to Belize, where Mr. Smith had arranged new names and passports for them. Then they were headed to a honeymoon suite in Aruba for a week and would retire to a new home on an island off the coast of Venezuela. Charles had shown her pictures of the white stucco house on the hill, overlooking the ocean, just yards away from the turquoise water and silver beach. No more hiding their affair, no more dealing with idiots at the law firm, no more Dominic, no more unpaid bills, deadlines, office politics, or frozen Colorado winters.

She wanted to tell everyone she had the flu, right now, and stay home for three days and leave without ever seeing anyone in the office building ever again. But she had to hang in there a little while longer.

"I know, I know." He rose from his chair.

She nodded and stood. They walked slowly to the door, and he opened it for her. She moved past Cindy's desk and into the hall, then looked back. Charles smiled his warmest smile, the one that melted her heart, but she suddenly remembered the word Cindy had used earlier about buying tickets: that "we" could get better ones.

Why would she be getting any kind of tickets for Charles and her?

CHAPTER 34

Parker opened his eyes and lay still, a restless dream turning ghostly, slipping quickly from his memory. An aluminum coffee pot was tucked into glowing embers inside the fire ring. A plastic poncho covered his body. Relic sat across from the burned-out fire, hugging his knees, eyes searching beyond their rocky shelter.

Parker waited for Relic to speak, but instead the man turned and poured what smelled like fresh coffee from the pot into a thermal mug and offered it.

"Thanks." Parker slid his arms from under the poncho, pushing and jostling himself into a seated position. His muscles felt like fresh leather left to dry in the sun. He took the well-worn mug.

"You bet," Relic mumbled.

Parker scratched his head and took a sip of the hot, bitter drink. Beyond their shelter and a dozen feet below lay a stretch of dry drainage. The flat, sandy bottom snaked its way beyond a bend in the arroyo and out of sight. Sheer sandstone cliffs rose several hundred feet above the canyon floor. He wondered what time it was but remembered that the gunmen had taken his phone. Maybe it didn't really matter, anyway.

Relic searched his pack and handed a piece of beef jerky to Parker. "It's not much, but it'll fill the void."

"I'll take it." Parker nodded and tore into the beef.

Relic stood and pulled a fresh length of bandage from his pack. "Okay to change it?"

"Yes, thank you." Parker nodded. He pulled his shirt away from the old bandage and unwound it. A nasty gash ran across and down the back of his shoulder, the flesh on either side red and puffy. Because of the angle of it, he couldn't see the injury below the curve of his shoulder.

"That's gonna leave a nice scar." Relic opened a tube of antibiotic cream and dribbled it across the shredded skin then gently wrapped the clean bandage over and around his shoulder blade.

"Better than the alternative."

"I've been thinking about what you said last night," Relic began.

"Hmmph?" His mouth was full.

"The place you work for—Sapphire Solutions—

owns some so-called holding company and a bunch of property, right?"

"Um-hmmph."

"So maybe they have the lease on the old oilfield, too, the one on Moonshine Mesa."

Parker squinted his eyes.

"It's the plateau above us."

Parker swallowed. "I think the oilfield is called Smoky Dome."

"Okay. And your pals Betty and Charles are in control of either the holding company owned by Sapphire Solutions, or in control of Sapphire Solutions itself."

"Or both. Right."

"And fifty-five million dollars gets transferred to the holding company in the next day or two?"

"Yes."

"But we don't know why they're transferring all that money?"

"Well, I think to expand the pump station," Parker said. "But whatever the reason for the payment, the pressure gauges need to read higher than they actually do."

"It's important—so important, that you think Betty hired some goons to kill you and Dom for finding out about the pressure readings?"

"That's the only reason I can think of."

Relic tugged on his goatee. "They don't want Global whatever to find out about the actual pressure on those pumps."

"So, why is the pressure so low?" Parker asked. "And Dom thought the pipes around the pumps were unusual. Something about the size of them being odd. And he'd worked in an oilfield years ago." Parker took a swallow of coffee, the caffeine beginning to sharpen his mind.

"Are they pumping oil up there?" Relic said.

"Great question."

"You feeling good enough today to move on?"

"Other than the shoulder, I'm okay. I don't feel so feverish this morning."

"Good. We need to get moving." Relic scooped sand into his hands and spread it over the embers. He refilled Parker's mug then poured the remainder of the coffee into the fire pit. He was packed and ready to go minutes later.

Parker downed more of the hot drink and leaned against the rock wall to help himself stand. His shoulder throbbed when he moved it.

"Where to?" Parker asked.

"Down this gorge to the river. We need water soon and there might be people at the Cedar Flute ruins who could help."

"We can get there from here?"

"Yep. Follow this drainage to the main canyon along the river. Down from there a couple of miles are the ruins. There's a dirt road to them. Part of the ruins are being reconstructed and there's an archeological dig nearby."

"So, there should be people there."

"If it's not off-limits as a crime scene."

"Crime scene?"

"I forgot to tell you. I found a dead man there a couple of days ago."

"And you forgot to tell me?"

Relic shrugged. "We've been busy. Plus, I didn't think it could be related."

"Yeah…" Parker thought about that for a moment. "But if it's a crime scene, there should be cops there who can help us."

"That's true, there might be. We can check it out. But there's not a lot of police manpower here in the outback."

"What happened with the dead man? You just found him?"

"Yep. Some kids who looked like college students showed up where I found the body and I decided to take off. I don't know what killed the guy."

"You didn't see anything else?"

"Nope. Lips were bluish, though, like he'd suffocated. But no wounds on the guy and no footprints around other than his. No signs of a fight. Very weird."

"That is weird." Parker rubbed his shoulder absentmindedly.

"And another thing." Relic raised a finger in the air. "Dead bees. Lots of them, and a dead crow. No reason for them to be dead, just lay'n there on the ground."

Talk about something unrelated, Parker thought.

"I found the crow and the dead man when I was following the string of dead bees."

"That's beyond weird," Parker said.

Relic scattered the fire ring and covered the soot with more dust and sand, then looked around their camp. He pulled his pack onto his back and began walking away.

Parker could hardly tell they'd slept there last night, had a little fire, drank gin, or had coffee for breakfast. He followed Relic out of the shade and into the light when Relic suddenly stopped and raised his arm.

Parker stood still for a moment, then he heard it too.

Someone was higher in the gorge, quickly stomping in their direction.

CHAPTER 35

Dawson pushed himself into a seated position and rubbed the back of his neck. He'd heard a "snap" last night that had twisted his nerves, but then the plateau had turned deeply silent, stars cast across the depth of space, and he'd fallen asleep.

He rubbed his fingers over the blood crusted along his pants leg, folding the surface here and there, feeling for wetness. Moisture on his outer thigh concerned him, but at least it seemed to have congealed.

The arc of the sun told him it was mid-morning. He needed to get back to the pump station and to the supplies in his jeep. He lifted his pistol, checked the slide, and released the magazine. Seventeen bullets. Pathetic, he thought. He hadn't even fired one shot toward his attacker. He reinserted the mag and rested the gun on his lap. At least the shelter he'd found kept him shaded, a real blessing in this desert heat.

A faint buzzing sound rose in his ears. He had no water left and one more energy bar, which he thought he should save for later. Or had he eaten it already?

He knew that moving might re-open the wound, but he'd never know unless he tried. He placed his Glock on the ground.

He rolled to his left, tucking his good leg underneath him. Using a ledge for support, he lifted himself about two feet up, scooting both legs under his hips. Gently, he stood more erect, testing his injured leg. It ached like the devil, and he had to use one arm on the rock to support himself. Could he get all the way to the jeep?

The sound in his head increased an octave, and he realized it was not a phantom in his mind but something real in the air above him. He shifted and searched the sky.

A tiny dot, dark against the blue, floated towards him, the sound now clearly that of a small airplane.

He unpinned the badge on his shirt and rubbed it clean. Judging the angle of the sun against the plane, he rotated the badge to flash it toward the pilot.

Come on come on come on.

The aircraft flew closer, a high-wing Cessna maybe, red under the wings, but its path was skirting his position. He waved and shouted, impossible gestures, he knew, and he flashed the badge again and again toward the little plane, but the constant buzz remained the same, no slowing, no variation, as the craft flew past him to the south.

The pilot had not seen him.

He dropped his arm to the side and rested against the ledge, defeat weighing on his bones like concrete.

His pant leg felt freshly wet, and when he looked, he could see new seepage above his knee.

"Damn it." He slid awkwardly to the ground, keeping his injured leg as straight as he could, the exertion making him dizzy.

He wasn't going anywhere.

Yesterday, he'd told Grace not to worry about him; that he'd be bushwacking across the plateau. But Grace and Rowe would begin to wonder about him later today. They'd check his phone and radio, maybe call his friends, even run to his house, all pissed off that he hadn't checked in. By the end of the day, though, they'd be really worried. They'd be in high gear by tomorrow.

He was going to have to wait for help and it stabbed at his ego like a frozen ice pick.

CHAPTER 36

Relic waved at him to follow. Parker soon realized that he was treading from rock to rock wherever he could, probably to minimize their footprints. Their movements masked the sound of whoever was in the canyon behind them, but the man must still be moving toward them. Parker knew he needed to step quickly. The gunman must have found a way from the pump station into the gorge. Maybe the one called "Wicks," the hollow-faced man, had hiked from where the canyon began as a shallow gully.

Parker held on to the mug of coffee, stopping for a second now and then to get more of the warm drink into him. They hiked briskly down a steep incline and stopped.

"Let me see your shoes," Relic said.

Parker lifted one to display the rubber sole.

"It'll do," Relic reached his palm toward the mug, beckoning with his fingers. Parker put his foot back on the ground, finished the coffee, and handed it to Relic. He fastened it to the outside of his pack with a carabiner.

"Why look at my shoes?" Parker asked.

"That guy who's following us?"

"Yes?"

"I'm betting he's not a climber. I'm betting he's wearing indoor shoes."

"Dress shoes?"

"Yep. You 'on board'?" His lips rose in a half-grin.

"This is no time for nautical jokes," Parker scolded.

"I love nautical jokes in the desert." Relic waved his hand toward the sand. "Besides, if you can't learn to laugh at trouble, you're never going to have much fun."

Parker rolled his eyes.

"Let's lead him somewhere interesting." Relic took them up a steep incline to what looked like a game trail of some kind, maybe one used by mountain sheep. The path took them along the cliffs, curving left, then right, then on a gentle rise to an expanse of solid sandstone. The main canyon stretched along their right side.

Relic stopped at the base of a convex curve of stone. "Catch your breath for a minute. Then we'll go up this slickrock."

Parker rested his hands on his knees. "Why do they call it that?"

"The white pioneers called it that when they crossed with their horses. The iron horseshoes slipped on the sandstone. Especially when it was wet."

Parker nodded.

The fall of a rock sounded behind them, close by.

"Time to go." Relic waved them forward and up the solid stone.

Parker leaned toward the angled rock, hands close to the ground as he went. They rose quickly for about twenty feet and the formation leveled out. Relic held his arms out from his sides as if to balance and Parker stood erect behind him.

"Follow me closely." Relic moved ahead, his steps short and measured.

Parker walked easily for several steps when the ground disappeared to his left, a giant gash in the ledge between where they were walking and the cliffs beyond. To his right, the rock dropped just as suddenly, down, down to the bottom of the canyon.

"Relic…"

"Follow in my steps," he said.

Parker took three more steps forward. The ledge dropped sharply into the rough rock hundreds of feet below, pulling his guts down with it. His head spun for a moment and he tried to focus on his shoes, something, anything close at hand. He raised his arms the way Relic had, his left shoulder aching, but the motion helped his sense of balance.

He slid one foot in front of the other, afraid to raise them from the ground. Relic had stopped about thirty yeads ahead and turned around.

Parker stopped.

"You can do it. It's not physical," Relic insisted. "It's just mental."

No shit.

"Don't psyche yourself out. Just keep walking."

Parker heard the man scrambling up the slickrock behind them.

Parker shuffled ahead. The path had to be about one yard wide, but it felt impossibly narrow, shrunken by the vast spaces that dropped on either side.

The gunman released a loud "humph," the exclamation a rousing shout in Parker's ear, sharp and close at hand. Parker stole a quick glance behind him. The man had fallen to the ground but was working to recover. He could see that it was Wicks. Parker shuffled more quickly now, crossing the slim beam of stone as it seemed to soar across the open air. Don't look, don't look.

Relic was closer now, dropped lower on the horizon, only his head visible above the rock.

Pop!

Wicks had shot at him! Parker's body jolted forward, now bent at the waist, his hands shaking, lifting his feet this time, striding forward on blind hope and faith that he'd stay on this slender slickrock ledge all the way across without falling to his death. He took one shallow breath and then another and another, faster and faster and sooner than he'd expected, the rock widened and sloped gently downward, and he slid to a stop with Relic's help.

They peered back across the ledge, but the hollow-faced man had slid back down the opposite end of the narrow bridge.

Parker gasped for breath, turning left and right, as if the motion would help. Relic patted him on the back and slowly he regained his air and his sense of solid ground beneath him.

"Told you," Relic said.

"What?" Parker panted.

"Indoor shoes."

Wicks could barely get partway up the slickrock, let alone dare to cross the upper part of the slickrock ledge.

"Come on." Relic waved them forward. "He'll have to go back down the long way. We gained some time, but that guy seems pretty determined…"

Yeah, Parker thought. Determined to finish them off.

CHAPTER 37

After some persuasion from Rowe, Will Cobb had agreed to come to the sheriff's office for an interview after three o'clock. She left the witness room door open and hobbled to the chair behind a wide, metal table. Dawson was who-the-hell-knew-where, chasing his moonshining hermit again, but Rowe didn't mind filling in for him. It was better than sitting around like an invalid, swollen ankle propped on a pillow. At least it was her left foot, so she could still drive.

Several minutes later, she heard a commotion in the front office, sounds of greetings and doors swinging open and shut. Grace peeked around the door and announced the arrival of the archeology student.

Will stepped into the room, a young man with toothpick arms and legs attached to a central body that seemed to toss his limbs to where they were needed. Curly black hair hung part way over tortoiseshell glasses with thick lenses that blurred his hazel eyes. He dropped a daypack to the floor and reached across to shake her hand.

"Thank you for coming in," Rowe said.

"Sure," he mumbled and sat across from her.

"You were a student in Professor Hollins's class, right?"

"The clinic, the practicum."

"Cedar Flute site?"

"Yes." He folded his hands in front of him.

"You're an archeology major?"

"Minor. My major is history."

She nodded and glanced at the notes Dawson had put in the file. "You've had classes from Professor Hollins in the past?"

"Yes." He brushed some dust from his pants.

This one was no chatterbox. "Deputy Dawson spoke with you at the scene the other day and we needed some follow up, if that's alright with you?" She smiled at Will, who did not react.

"I'll get right to the point." She tapped her finger on the papers in front of her. "You had a run-in with Professor Hollins last semester?"

He shifted in his seat. "What do you mean?"

"Well, we understand that he accused you of stealing an artifact from the site. An accusation that almost got you expelled."

Will nudged his glasses higher up his nose and shook his head. "I never stole any artifacts."

"So, the professor's accusation was baseless?"

"Yes, most certainly." He nodded, relieved to have some understanding of the matter from the deputy.

"What happened?"

"A flint knife was found at the site, then went missing. Made of red chert, actually." He looked her in the eye. "I didn't take it."

"Who did?"

"I don't know!" He raised his voice. "Hollins accused me of it and reported it to the board." He took a breath. "Shit. I didn't take the damn thing. But I had to defend myself and Hollins nearly had me kicked out of school."

"Nearly?"

"The board voted. There was no proof, so they reinstated my status."

Rowe leaned toward him. "That would have really pissed me off."

"Well, yeah, I was pissed."

"So then, why take another course, or another clinic, with Hollins?"

"He's the professor in charge of the dig at Cedar Flute. I graduate this year, but I need the credits from a clinic. It's the only project they've got going right now."

"You had no choice but to take the course, to have contact again with Hollins?"

"Yes, but I didn't kill him."

"Whoa there, Will. I didn't say you did."

"That's where you're going with this, isn't it? Angry student kills professor?" His heel rose and fell against the floor, a jittery tap.

"Since you've brought the conversation to this point, why don't you tell me. Did you kill Professor Hollins?"

CHAPTER 38

They followed another game trail for a long time and then wound around several low boulders, dropping closer to the center of the drainage. Relic kept a grueling pace and had to stop every few yards to let Parker catch up. At least they weren't on the edge of some precipice, he thought. Solid ground around his feet reassured him that he was not going to spin into oblivion. Not at the moment, at least.

They stopped at a turn in the twisting canyon and listened but heard nothing.

Relic led them farther and farther down the gorge as it widened and gently eased to more level ground. The sound of rushing water met them at the mouth of the canyon and Relic hurried even faster to a grove of box elder trees by the river.

Parker glanced behind them. Walls of red rock blocked his view of the sky, chunks of stone carved downward with a ragged blade. He bent at the waist, catching his breath, then followed Relic to the water.

Relic had filled a collapsible bucket and set it on the riverbank. He pulled a plastic tube and filter from his pack and began pumping water from the bag into one of the near-empty water bottles. When that was full, he did the same with the other water bottle and set it aside. Then he slipped an empty bladder from his pack and began filling it as well.

"Can I help?" Parker knelt next to him.

"Keep pumping. When this is full, put it into my pack. Then drink all you can from one of the water bottles and fill it again." Relic handed him the small pump and filter. "I'm going to look around. See if I can see that guy."

Parker nodded and began pumping their water into the large bladder. His arms were tired within minutes and he had to stop now and then to rest, his shoulder aching from the exertion. He was wearing out already and it was only mid-morning.

Relic returned and squatted next to Parker. "I can hear him, but he's a ways behind us. Here." He took the pump from him and resumed his efforts much more efficiently than Parker's. In moments, the bladder was full. Relic slid it into his pack, now especially full and heavy.

Then he and Parker took long drinks from the bottles and topped them off. Relic collapsed the portable bucket and squeezed it and the filter into his pack. The rope he'd used to help Parker was still fastened to the outside of the rucksack.

They hurried through the trees, back toward the high cliffs, and angled downriver.

They were beyond the shade now and Parker could feel the heat of the sun on his neck, sweat running down his armpits. They kept going, and going, but at least the walking was level. They passed a narrow slot canyon on their left and found a weak trail, of sorts, following the contours of the cliffs above.

"Hey," Parker panted, stopping for another break.

Relic turned and watched him, breaths even and relaxed. The man must do this kind of running all day long to stay in shape. And Parker had to be half his age. Maybe even a third. With Relic, it was hard to tell.

Parker regained enough oxygen to start again, and they rounded a curve to more open ground. They passed a large rock on their left and turned left again. Parker stopped.

Yellow crime scene tape was anchored to the ground with rocks in a rough trapezoid formation. The center of the area was empty, but the message was clear:

someone had died here. Recently.

"This is…" Parker heaved his breath.

"Yep. This is where I found that guy dead. And over there," he pointed behind him, "was a dead crow. The bees and the crow, that's what led me here."

"They led you here?"

"I was following a trail of death, so to speak, when I found the man's body." Relic nodded toward the yellow tape. "They've gotta be connected…"

Parker sat cross-legged onto the sandy soil, exhausted.

"Can't stop now," Relic said. "We need to get around these ruins."

Parker saw a single stone room tucked into the bluff, its doorway black as night. Relic saw him looking and said, "That's the mother-in-law suite. Set back from the rest of them."

"What's past the ruins?"

"A way back up to the plateau."

"You're shitting me," Parker said, regretting it immediately. "I mean, I'm played out, here, man. We've gotta go back up again?"

"The man with the gun is not far behind."

"For real?"

"I'd say a half mile. With any luck, he doesn't know

he's this close to us. But if he does, he'll be hurrying now. We couldn't hide our tracks completely."

"Shit."

"My sentiments exactly." Relic waved Parker forward.

He stood slowly and rubbed the long scab forming on his shoulder. "Okay, okay."

They rounded another curve in the cliffs and a complex of rooms and paths and walls opened before them, anchored on the far side by a tall, circular tower. Sandstone blocks had been carved, stacked, and cemented with mud into a labyrinth of houses and alleys.

Wooden boxes and shovels lay on the ground near a long, rectangular hole in the earth. The archeological dig Relic had told him about, abandoned for now. A dirt road angled away from the site, over a rise, and out of sight.

"Hey, we could take the road, right?" Parker asked.

"We'd be out in the open for miles."

"But there might be help out there."

"Not likely," Relic pointed. "See those orange street cones?"

Parker saw a row of them near the rise.

"I'd guess the sheriff has made the whole area a crime scene," Relic said. "No one coming down here anytime soon."

"Unless it's the sheriff himself."

"True. You want to take that chance? That he'd be on this remote road sometime today?"

"Well…"

Relic held a finger to his lips. Parker looked behind them and there, shuffling around the bend in the cliffs a quarter mile away, was the gunman who'd shot him.

"Shit," Parker forced the words through his teeth.

Just then, the hollow-faced man looked up and saw them.

CHAPTER 39

"No!"

"You were there at the site," Rowe said. "You could have left your station for a few minutes, done it without anyone noticing you, and gone back."

"No," Will put his fists on the tabletop. "Ask any of the others. I was on grid seventeen the whole time. Focused on the digging. We heard Keith yelling something and a couple of us got up and ran to see. Hollins was on the far side of the ruins, out of everyone's sight."

She folded her arms across her chest and watched him from under her brow.

"Really. I don't know who killed the man."

"You wanted to, though, didn't you?"

"No. Well, sure, the guy's an ass and he nearly ruined my career path, that's true." He stopped tapping his foot. "But the board over-ruled him. I'll graduate at the end of this semester. With honors."

"And?"

"Why would I mess that up?" He slumped in his chair and stared at the wall, brooding.

Fair question, she thought. "Revenge?"

Will waved a hand at her, dismissing the notion. "I'm out of there in a few more weeks and never looking back."

Could this skinny nerd really have suffocated Professor Hollins? There were no obvious signs of struggle. Which meant his attacker would have to have overpowered him quickly.

"Okay. Give me the names of students near you at the time, before Keith called you over. People who might verify that you stayed on your task instead of wandering around."

Will kept his eyes on the wall. "Keith Simmons. Rob and Susan, I forget their last names. Your deputy has them. The driver from the college. He drives one of the vans but doesn't help with the dig. If he was watching us, he'd have seen me there the whole time."

"Driver?" She didn't see that in Dawson's notes.

"Yeah. Older guy."

Someone who could explore the site without responsibility for the dig or the students? Someone else with an opportunity to kill the professor?

Shit. The case seemed to lead from one dead end to another. But she'd call the driver in for questioning and see what happened next.

CHAPTER 40

The Cedar Flute ruins rested on a long slab of sandstone fifteen feet above where Parker and Relic stood. Bluffs rose above and overhung the ruins another five or six hundred feet to the plateau, sheltering the complex. The weathered cliffs were streaked with desert varnish, minerals leached from the stone over eons, staining the face like blackened tears.

Relic began a quick climb to the base of the pueblo buildings. Parker leaned forward, into the rise, to help propel himself upward. After three dozen painful steps to the top, he had to stop to rest.

"Almost there," Relic encouraged him.

Panting, he turned to look for the gunman. The man was crossing open ground, closing on them.

Still out of breath, Parker struggled the last few feet to the top of the base, where the bedrock leveled out and the ruins began. Relic waved him forward again, past the first set of waist-high walls and across an open area. To their left stood a neat, flat façade with three windows and a doorway on the main floor and three windows on a second story. Remnants of log floor beams protruded from below the upper windows, toothpicks hanging loosely from a slackened mouth. A large, circular kiva was carved into the ground to their right, stone walls partly fallen into the center.

They passed a solid wall of chiseled stone and reached the end, its corner a perfect, ninety-degree edge. They hid behind it, Parker breathing heavily.

Relic moved along another façade about seven feet high with two open doorways, the bottom thirds narrower than the upper portions, as if creatures with wide torsos and narrow legs had to fit through them. He moved to another wall that was perpendicular to the façade, the outer portion crumbled to the ground. He picked his way through the fallen stones and looked back at Parker.

"Coming," he whispered, willing himself to hurry.

Relic disappeared behind the crumbling wall.

Pop!

A pistol echoed beneath the sandstone overhang, startling Parker into a run.

Pop, pop!

A spot of sand burst from the ground to Parker's

right. He heaved his body forward, thighs burning, ankles weak from exhaustion, and he turned the corner and was suddenly behind the broken wall with Relic. They'd entered a crumbling building, out of the line of fire.

"This way." Relic stepped carefully over fallen stones and behind another wall that took them deep into the shadows. They moved to one of those oddly shaped doorways and stepped slowly through, touching the sides as they went. Outdoors again, they went to another structure, the walls a semi-circle of stone. It was the tower he'd seen from below the ruins.

Relic slipped through the doorway and into the hollow column.

Pop!

Parker saw the hollow-faced man, maybe thirty yards away, feet planted in the ground, both arms straight and level. For a split second, Parker couldn't move, couldn't breathe, couldn't think.

Relic leaned out of the tower and grabbed Parker's arm, twisting his wound in the effort, pain dragging him out of his stupor, and he lurched sideways and through the stone doorway and onto the dusty floor with a heavy "humph." He scrambled to his feet, resting against the inner wall, the air rasping past his vocal cords.

Relic peeked outside the door.

"You're cornered now," Wicks shouted. "You're trapped in there."

Parker heard him shuffling outside.

"Come out now and we'll talk about all of this."

Relic shook his head.

Parker searched for another doorway or window but all he saw was a decrepit pair of logs leaning against the stone, remnants of a wooden ladder to a second story that had rotted away hundreds of years ago.

"Come out now or I'll come in shooting."

CHAPTER 41

Deputy Rowe propped her left heel on the office radiator and massaged her foot through the bandages. Her bruised muscles alternated between itching her to madness and hurting like hell. Then, they'd be fine for several hours. She couldn't seem to predict what they were going to do next.

Joshua DuBose was a driver for the university and had transported students to the Cedar Flute site the day Professor Hollins had been found dead. Will Cobb had told her that the driver could have seen Hollins because DuBose usually stayed in the large van or wandered around by himself, separate from the students working on the dig. Rowe didn't find anything in Dawson's notes about DuBose, so she'd arranged for him to come to the office for an interview.

She wiggled her foot back into its boot, leaving the laces open.

Grace leaned into the room. "DuBose is here. Show him in?"

Rowe nodded.

A large male, six foot two and maybe two hundred and sixty pounds, pushed his way past Grace as she shut the door. In his late fifties, everything about him seemed rounded at the edges: his shoulders, nose, cheeks, eyes, even the bottoms of his ear lobes. He held a baseball cap in his hand and walked to Rowe's desk.

"Officer Rowe?"

"Nice to meet you." She stood and they shook hands. The man was definitely strong enough to have strangled Professor Hollins. "Thanks for coming in. We've been talking to everyone at the ruins the day the professor died and you're part of that list."

"Sure." He sat in the chair across from her.

"Can I get you any coffee?"

"No, thanks." His eyes seemed to dart across the room like a water skipper, landing then jerking away from her diploma, academy photo, desk phone, her statue of a pig with wings.

She ran him though the basics: how long he'd worked at the university, what his duties included, whether he knew Hollins or any of the students outside of the campus. A widower, he shared a house with an old friend, enjoyed being around the students, and kept to himself. He seemed genuinely surprised when she asked if he'd ever had any disagreements with Hollins.

"I only knew him from the college, and not even much from that. I mean, he'd call to schedule the van and I'd take them to the site unless another driver got assigned. We'd talk some during the drive, you know? But nothing serious."

"Did you mind going there, all the way out to the site?"

"No. It's a dusty drive, but pretty. Once we were there, Hollins never cared much what I did. So, I'd read, or listen to music, or even take a quick nap until the students were done. Sometimes I'd drive all the way back to campus and then come back for them, but not usually. It's a fair distance out there and back, so it takes a while. Those kids are pretty tuckered out by the end of the day, too, I can tell you that..."

Rowe slid her foot from the boot and scratched it against the bottom of her other one. "Sorry," she said, wiggling a bit with the effort. "Itchy foot."

"Sure." His eyes settled on her bookcase, scanning from one row to the next.

"Did you see anyone with the professor right before they found him?

Anything that day that might help us?"

"Yeah, I did."

She stopped scratching. "What?"

"I was stretching my legs some, walking north, or northwest, from the van and the dig. See," he leaned forward, "there's the main part of the ruins, where the dig is, then there's some more ruins around a bend in the cliffs. Separate."

"Yes?"

"I was, I don't know, less than a quarter mile away from those, but I saw one of the students leave the site and go toward the separate ruin. I've heard it called the mother-in-law suite because it's away from the rest of them. Anyway, I later found out that student was Keith Simmons."

"Yes?"

"Keith came round the corner and shouted something. That's when I saw another guy, older than the students, stand up from the ground. Keith came at him with a shovel, the other guy dodged him and walked away. Keith fell down then three other students came over to him. That's when the commotion really heated up, 'cause the others started yelling and they all came to the same spot, in front of the mother-in-law suite. I came over to see what was going on and that's when I also saw Professor Hollins, dead on the ground. One of the other students had called for emergency help by the time I got there, but it was obvious the professor was dead."

Rowe peppered him with questions, but he seemed to have no information beyond what he'd explained, which added nothing to what Keith and the other students had already reported.

Mr. DuBose couldn't describe the man who ran from the site beyond saying that he had a pack on his back, seemed to be older than the students, and was average height and weight.

Then Grace slid through the office door and handed Rowe a print-out that could change the equation entirely.

CHAPTER 42

"You go first," Relic pointed toward what was left of the ancient ladder.

"That ladder's not going to get us anywhere," Parker said.

"You got to the count of ten," yelled the man outside.

"I mean—" Relic began.

"We're not getting out of this alive," Parker's words blew from his lungs with a sense of desperation.

"Hey, now—nobody gets out of this life alive…" Relic said, but the humor was lost on Parker.

Relic moved behind the frail ladder and reached into the shadows behind it. "There's a passage here, an escape built into the design. The pueblo people had their enemies, just like us. Squeeze through, then up and over and you'll be out of the tower," he whispered.

"…five…" the man shouted.

Parker followed Relic's instruction, feeling his way through the dark, wiggling into a hole in the wall that allowed him to see light above. He scrambled over rocky debris, blocks fallen from the ruins, and reached a chokecherry bush anchored to the cliffs. He stretched his fingers around the trunk and pulled himself out of the tower completely, scooting in the dust to the other side of the bush.

Pop, pop, pop!

Relic's head rose from the dark opening, and he climbed quickly past Parker and along a narrow ledge of solid rock. Parker followed, balancing against the face of the cliff. The ledge dropped sharply to his right, a hundred and fifty feet to the rugged ground below. He slowed, shuffling his feet along the edge, running his hands along the rock face for balance. Eventually, they reached a large, rounded boulder that seemed to replace the sheer cliff on their left.

"Step up," Relic cupped his hands in front of him.

"Up there?" Parker stared at the smooth stone, wondering how quickly he could slide off and to his death.

"Once we're up this, we're safe," Relic said. "Promise."

"Yeah?" Parker's knees felt rubberized, his muscles pushed to their limit, but they couldn't stand here on this thin shelf forever. He put his right foot in Relic's hands and when he stood, Relic lifted him upward, heaving him to a spot where the giant rock leaned away from the abyss. His weight held him against the stone as he scrambled to where it leveled off. He turned and waited.

"Grab this." Relic unshouldered his pack and threw it, shotput style, up the curving rock. Parker grabbed the handle on top, dragging it toward his feet. Relic took a quick breath and jumped, fingers scratching along the top, pulling, scooting, jostling awkwardly higher until he reached Parker's level spot. They pushed onward on their rear ends, sliding, lifting with their arms, then sliding again until they reached the downward slope on the other side of the rock. Relic leapt to the ground, legs absorbing his momentum. Parker slid the pack to him. He scootched as far down the boulder as he could, each step holding him by friction alone, his legs more and more directly underneath him. When it seemed that he could scramble no farther, he jumped to the ground next to Relic.

"I knew you could do it." Relic patted him on the back.

"Where are we?" Parker stood slowly.

"We're on what some people call an old Moki, or Pueblo, trail. Built by the Pueblo people who lived here."

Relic turned and waved toward a set of steps ground into solid rock, curving up and out of sight. "That boulder has been there a long time, cutting off this trail. If you don't know where it is, or can't get over the boulder, you can't reach this spot."

"How is this even here?" Parker craned his neck upward at the rising steps and that simple motion released a wave of vertigo.

"The ancestors carved these steps a thousand years ago. By hand."

Parker caught his reference to ancestors but was too dizzy to ask.

"This takes us all the way to the plateau." Relic grinned.

Parker sat and released a low groan.

"But for now, we rest right here. We'll eat and get some water into us."

CHAPTER 43

Betty scanned the financial reports for the first quarter, some of her projections directly on point, others off base. The insurance budget was spent for the whole year, but she knew those bills came due in February; there would be no more expenses in that column until next year. Supplies were on track. Travel costs were too high for the quarter. The firm couldn't maintain that rate of spending all year and stay within the budget. Mileage reimbursements, hotels, airfare... The more she looked at the numbers, though, the more she had to pull away and try again. They just weren't staying in her head this afternoon.

She stopped trying.

Airfare. Tickets. Cindy saying "we" could find better "tickets." Charles said they were concert tickets for him and his niece, but... She knew it was nothing but her brain would not let it go.

She rubbed her pencil against the bottom of the report, thinking, worrying, smudging the page, and finally wearing right through the paper.

She and Charles had planned their retirement together for nearly nine months. Neither of them had a spouse, so neither was cheating on someone else, but they'd kept their relationship a secret at the office. In fact, for their plan to work, no one could suspect they would run off together. Their affair was on fire at first and then it had cooled to a steady burn, the kind to last a lifetime. They'd planned and schemed and designed together. They dreamed of a life of leisure and money, more than just financial security—the means to travel the world in style. Charles had found a way to turn it into reality. He'd set Betty up as the CFO of Sapphire Solutions. He'd found a massive grant to expand a climate change mitigation project out on Smoky Dome. Converting the old oilfield into a unique storage project had been genius. Once the funds were deposited to a holding company, Charles would transfer them to several faux contractors set up with help from Mr. Smith. From there, the funds would go to an offshore account.

They were in love. It was going to be a retirement by royalty. Their first year, alone, they would travel to Italy, Spain, and Greece.

In three days, she would be on a scheduled vacation. Charles would pretend to fall ill with Covid and cancel all his appointments, then disappear.

She was overthinking that little remark by Cindy, wasn't she? After all, Charles had explained it.

Someone knocked on her door.

"Come in." She put her hands over the hole she'd worn in the paper.

Cindy seemed to prance into the office, blonde hair bouncing against her shoulders. "Staff meeting agenda for next week," she said, placing a sheet on Betty's desk. Some of the older law partners still wanted agendas printed before the meetings and preparing them was one of Charles's—and therefore Cindy's—tasks. The young woman spun briskly away, her back to Betty as she swayed through the door and out of the office. She seemed especially pleased with herself today. It had taken her less than ten seconds to deliver the agenda and scoot back out the door. Too damn perky.

Charles had kept his and Betty's relationship a complete secret for months. No one suspected it. Was he keeping another relationship secret, too?

CHAPTER 44

DuBose sat quietly while Deputy Rowe scanned the papers that Grace had delivered. Grace had been smart to check DuBose's record, which showed two separate arrests for assault by the university driver. The arrests were old— thirty-eight years ago—but they showed the man's capacity to violently attack another person.

She straightened in her chair, her injured, itchy foot all but forgotten.

"I need to ask you, Mr. DuBose, about a couple of arrests you've had." She looked into his round blue eyes, her statement simple and direct.

The man blinked.

"Want to tell me what happened? Your side of the story?" She set the police records on her desk, where he could see them, too.

"Oh, for god's sake." DuBose rolled his eyes at the ceiling. "Yes, yes, of course." He pulled on one of his earlobes.

"Yes?"

"You're right. I had two arrests, over thirty years ago. Back then…" he scooted forward on his chair. "You have to understand. I was drinking back then. I got into an argument with a friend. We were in a bar in Denver, and, well, we'd been drinking pretty much all day. By midnight, I think we'd both hit some kind of a brick wall. He made a snide remark about a woman I was interested in. I made a swipe at him, not really serious, you know, but then he took one at me. He missed, but it made me mad and then I took a real swing and hit him, square in the nose. Blood all over the table. Bar tender tossed us both out on the street where the police were waiting."

DuBose clasped his hands on his lap. "We were both drunk. When we finally sobered up, my pal refused to press charges."

"I see." She tilted her head. "And the other assault?"

He shook his head as if it could rid him of the memory. "Like I say, I was still drinking in those days. A couple of months later, some guy I'd just met got in a wrestling match with me. God, we were falling-down drunk. I don't know how anyone figured which one of us started it and, to this day, I don't remember."

"You were both arrested?"

"Yeah. This time, the judge gave me a choice: hard time or treatment. I got sober, finally." He looked up at her. "I've been sober now for thirty-eight years, four months, and…five days."

She stared at the old police records from Colorado. Two very old assault charges, both of which had been dismissed. Both of which had involved dangerous amounts of alcohol. Today, the man was thirty-eight years sober.

"Good work on your recovery." She looked up at him.

"I think of it as an addiction in remission."

"Right. Listen, I had to ask."

"Sure." He nodded. "I get it. But I had nothing to do with Professor Hollins's death and I didn't see it happen."

"Yeah." She scratched her brow.

Sheriff Leavitt already figured the professor's death was natural, or at least accidental. Deputy Dawson was pursuing the missing witness, the ponytail man he claimed was responsible for all kinds of mischief over the years. Rowe was skeptical of either conclusion, but one thing was clear about this investigation.

She was back to square one.

CHAPTER 45

"It's only the finest trail food ever devised." Relic handed him a baggie full of peanut M&M's. "A cure for just about anything."

Parker took a handful and returned the bag. "I'm exhausted."

"How's your shoulder?"

"Hurts about as bad as the rest of me."

"Perfect."

Parker canted his head the way a dog asks a question.

"Means you're fighting off the infection and it's no worse than any other part of you anymore."

Relic has a different way of seeing things, Parker thought, but then, maybe that's what keeps him alive out here. They ate the candy followed by two strips of jerky each and plenty to drink. The water tasted like it had been boiled with old wool socks, but he was grateful for it.

"There's a broad shelf near the top where we can camp at tonight. Some wood around for a fire, I think." Relic stood.

Parker thought it was way too soon to be climbing again, but getting to camp for the night was a tempting goal. He stood slowly, balancing on the rock as he went, legs whining for relief.

Relic led the way, stopping from time to time to let Parker catch up. As he went, his thighs and ankles seemed to go numb and the climb actually seemed a little easier. Or maybe it was a "mental" issue after all and he was doing a little better at it.

They stepped up and up and up, the exertion stealing his breath every few feet, but finally they reached a grassy area where erosion had carved a crescent of level ground out of the towering rocks. Parker stumbled beneath an overhang and plopped into the sand. Relic sat his pack by the rock and searched for loose stones, tossing them near Parker's feet. Then Relic disappeared around a corner.

Parker leaned forward and arranged the stones into a fire ring, of sorts. Not as neat as what Relic had done the night before, but it would do. Relic returned with a small armload of deadwood, laid it near the rocks, and left again, hiking out of sight. A few minutes later, he dragged a branch as thick as his leg over to the camping area and dropped it.

The heat of the day had begun to radiate away from the reddened earth, the sun dropping low on the horizon.

"Let's start a fire," Parker said.

"Soon as it's dark," Relic said. "Don't want anyone to see the smoke while it's light out."

Relic sat next to him, a few feet away, and they watched as cotton candy clouds turned red and purple, blushing with the setting sun. Distant cliffs seemed to rise and then evaporate in the haze, massive, immobile beasts from the days of the dinosaurs. He'd never seen anything as real or beautiful or moving in his whole life.

They munched on M&M's for a while, languishing in the sweet crunch of them, and Relic arranged the wood for a fire. Parker stood, stiff-legged, walked around the bend, and relieved his bladder. When he returned and sat down, he decided he would never stand up again—his legs were just too worn out.

Relic set one water bottle next to his climbing rope and one next to Parker. He rummaged through his daypack and pulled a small, red apple from one of the pockets and cut it in two. Where the hell had that come from? He handed half to Parker.

Never had an apple tasted so full of juice

and wonder.

Relic straightened the hair in his ponytail and squatted by the fire, the spitting image of early man, twenty thousand years ago. With a kernmantle alpine climbing rope. And McIntosh apples.

Colors quickly drained from the landscape, casting it in tones of sepia. Relic handed Parker his rain poncho and he wrapped himself in it to stay warm. He stared at the sand and grass at their little camp, thinking of Dom, the evil that had taken his life, watching dusk melt into night, wondering what the hell was going on.

CHAPTER 46

Parker cleared his throat. "Is there some connection between the dead bees you found and the dead man by the ruins and whatever Betty and Charles Story are doing up at the pump station?"

"I've been wondering the same thing. At first, I thought maybe some kind of bird flu had killed the crow, but the bees too? And that would not explain a man suffocating like that out in the open air."

Parker thought about the pumps and what Dom had said. He knew that oilfields pushed water and chemicals into geologic formations to squeeze the oil out, but Dom had said the pipes didn't look like the ones he'd seen when he worked in the oil fields. And he'd said no oil was being taken out of the ground at all. If he was right about that, why pump something into the ground?

He told this to Relic, who sat cross-legged by the fire, staring into that space where people look when they need to think.

"If you don't mind me asking, do you have any of that gin left?"

Relic nodded. "Not going to keel over again, are you?"

"Maybe. It's pretty good."

"My own blend."

"You made it? Like cooked it on a still or something?"

"Homemade hooch." He pulled the flask from his pack and poured some into the mug they'd used for coffee that morning.

"You're the G.O.A.T., you know?"

Relic stopped. "I'm a what?"

"You're the G.O.A.T."

"I can eat just about anything, but I don't see myself as a goat."

"Not a goat, the G.O.A.T."

"What's the difference?"

Parker stared at Relic for a moment, making sure he wasn't teasing him. "G.O.A.T. means greatest of all time. It's the initials, G-O-A-T."

"Oh, okay. Thanks, I guess…"

"How long have you been out here?"

"Not long enough."

"God, if I lived out here, I'd have F.O.M.O. big time."

Relic wrinkled his nose.

"Fear of missing out…"

"Of course." Relic rolled his eyes. "You'd 'batten down the hatches' then your GOAT would have a FOMO."

They shared a laugh.

"So…do you live near here?" Parker asked.

"Yep."

"Is your still nearby?"

"Not too far." He handed the flask to Parker.

"Thanks. Well…" Parker didn't want to pry; after all, the man had saved his ass more than once.

"To Dom." Relic raised the coffee mug.

"To Dom," Parker agreed, and they each took a swig of the moonshine. Parker held his hand to his throat and coughed.

"Were you and Dom close friends?"

"Friends?" The gin seemed to take a circular swim though his head. "No. We worked together but I've only known him a couple of weeks. But I liked him." The liquor warmed his stomach and loosened his muscles, feelings he relished in the moment.

They sat quietly. Parker took another shot of

homemade gin and shivered as the burn slid down his throat. He thought about three or four good friends from his schoolyard days, scattered across the country. "I don't have a lot of real friends." As soon as he'd said it, he hated the sound of self-pity in his voice. "Sorry. It's this damn gin," he said as he lifted the flask for another shot, embracing his own inconsistency.

"Me neither," Relic said.

"No, I mean I really don't fit in anywhere." He ran a finger through the sand at his feet.

"Loneliness won't leave you alone?" Relic looked at him from under his brow and grinned.

"Yeah, I guess." Parker smiled despite himself.

Relic nodded. "But you want to fit in."

"I guess I do. I mean, sure. I've been trying. My parents are estranged. I have no brothers. My only sister died two years ago. I had a girlfriend, but, really, she wanted me to convert to her religion and run around with her friends and we just didn't fit. We broke up."

"Different churches?"

"No church, really." He watched the fire flicker against Relic's weathered face, his eyes deeper, nose sharper in the harsh light.

"You know," Relic leaned forward, "most of what we think of as religion is really history. Or culture. Nothing wrong with that, of course, but it helps to remember what we're swimming in. Sometimes our assumptions do the talking for us, without even thinking. We get caught up in them and make them our very identity and that's when the trouble starts."

"Trouble?"

"Us versus them. One group against another." He shrugged. "It's human nature to want to be part of a group. But it can go too far. We define ourselves most sharply by identifying an enemy – Russians, Americans, Catholics, Muslims, whatever it might be. We sometimes use symbols to reinforce the idea that we are fundamentally separate and different from others, though that's not true. We fall in love with our own identities. Then we push them onto others, and that's the fuel for warfare."

"It's human nature to kill each other off," Parker grumbled, pointing to the wound in his shoulder.

"It's human nature to take things to the extreme," Relic agreed.

Parker took another swig of gin, fire dancing through the sticks, images dancing through his head. He thought again of Dom and the shooter and Cindy and Betty, of bullets from guns and poisons from drinks. "Human nature is a pain in the ass, you know?"

"You're telling me..." Relic laughed, his voice

deep and infectious. "It's best to drink upstream from the herd."

Parker poked the flames with a stick, releasing micro-stars into the cool night air. He watched each ember float into space and imagined galaxies forming around those tiny, fading suns.

"Welcome to the church of the great outdoors." Relic opened his arms, displaying their cozy shelter. "Membership includes all of the organisms that run around on this incredible planet, including us little humans."

"Yeah." Parker smiled at the thought.

"The simple fact that you are here means that you fit in—the fact that you exist is more than enough. And if you don't fit in very well with society, then to hell with that. I bet you connect better with other creatures, anyway. Horses. Dogs. Wild things. We are all born of the earth, and we all return to her. Feel that direct connection."

Parker nodded, then thought about his old girlfriend, a direct connection he had cut. "I'm tired of people trying to find spiritual experiences from a bunch of zealots. Religious salesmen..." Parker scrolled his finger through the dust.

"Identity salesmen." Relic nodded. "You know what I think?" He leaned forward. "In this world, we're not human beings in search of a spiritual experience." He let the words hang in the air. "Not at all."

"What are we, then?"

"We are spirits. And we are having a human experience."

"That kinda turns your perspective around." Parker stared into the flames.

"We cling to our expectations like life preservers. Hey…there's another nautical expression for you." A wide smile crossed Relic's face.

Parker wrinkled his nose. "So, what are you saying? You think we're making inaccurate presumptions about what's going on up on the mesa?"

"Maybe. In logic puzzles, it's our assumptions that lead us astray."

CHAPTER 47

Dawson listened and listened, a tiny hum in his ears the only sound he could detect. He slid his pistol back into its holster and scooted to a more comfortable position. He'd napped longer than he'd expected, shadows reaching toward his shelter like the lanky fingers of a piano maestro. Thirst had its desiccated grip on his throat and though part of him thought he should preserve some water for tomorrow, he drank the last of it in four long swallows, rich and glorious. It would have to last him.

He peeked beyond the rock wall and out across the plain. The sun had dropped more than he'd thought, the last rays illuminating the bottom of a distant, smeared-out cloud.

He thought about the supplies in his Jeep. Even if he tried again to get there, he realized that he could not reach it before dark. He'd waited too long for the western sun to be positioned in the gunman's eyes—it would be pitch black by the time he got halfway there. Would the dark make it easier to sneak past the gunman at the pump station? Why was he even thinking about this? He could barely stand up the last time he'd tried.

He could keep resting right here if he didn't get too cold. He searched for bits and scraps of wood and made a small pile in front of him. His leg began to throb but he powered through the pain, crawling on hands and knees outside the shelter. He found a large sagebrush with dead branches and hacked away at them with his hunting knife. He circled the area on hands and knees, searching. He found a few weathered pieces of wood the diameter of his wrist and toiled back to the rocky cove, pulling them behind.

He stacked the wood like a miniature log cabin, pieces laid one across the other, loose bark and grass in the center.

The sun dropped fully behind the horizon, leaving the plateau in an eerie purple glow.

He found two rocks the size of neck pillows and rolled them to the base of the woodpile. Once heated, they would cool slowly and help him stay warmer through the night. A little bit, anyway.

A stiff breeze swept past the shelter, shivering the grass. The scent of something rank touched his nose for a moment, then wafted away. He got as comfortable as he could, back against the rocky enclosure, his injured leg straight and flat against the sand. He'd torn open the wound, fresh blood soaking into the T-shirt he'd wrapped around it. He closed his eyes, exhaustion pulling him downward.

The snap of a broken twig made him stiffen. He pulled matches from his pocket and debated whether to start the fire now or wait until the cold was too much to bear.

Something moved in the dark, a flicker of shadow against the black. It wouldn't be the gunman this late at night, not without a flashlight. He reminded himself that it could be any number of harmless things. Fear nearly always arose from something specific; a real and concrete danger. But his antennae were up anyway, his nerves a fluttering bird with no place to land.

Suddenly, that scent returned—a wet, rank smell of raw meat and rancid hide, something specific to fear. He listened for any noise, any step on the ground, his heart quickening in his chest and then he saw them— two glassy eyes low to the ground, green and crouching, gliding deliberately closer to him.

CHAPTER 48

"This gin is getting to me, but I'd like another shot." Parker raised a brow. "Y.O.L.O. you know."

"What?"

"You only live once."

"We'd better eat something before you come up with another one." Relic searched the side pockets on his pack and pulled out a pair of granola bars. "G.B. for the G.O.A.T." Relic grinned, teeth white against his skin.

Parker groaned.

Relic handed a bar to Parker, who tore open the package with his teeth and took a large bite of it. Relic added wood to the fire, its warmth radiating across Parker's face and chest, his backside cool against the rock. He washed down the granola with a long drink of water.

Parker puzzled again about the pump station, the money going to Betty's company. The idea that the station was pushing something into the ground and nothing out.

He put the last of the granola in his mouth and reached for the papers Dom had given him, the pages ripped from Betty's confidential report. He turned toward the firelight, re-reading the documents.

Global Green Engineering was going to pay fifty-five million dollars to renovate and expand the Smoky Dome oilfield pumping station.

"What would someone pump into the ground?" Parker asked.

"It would have to be a liquid or a gas," Relic said. "Technically, under pressure, it can actually be both or can switch from one to the other."

"Gas…" Parker drew out the word.

"Yep," Relic said.

Parker leafed through the pages, searching. "Hey. There's a footnote here about what Global Green Engineering does as a business." He squinted to read the fine print. "They do carbon sequestration."

"Carbon…" Relic's voice trailed away.

Thoughts rattled in Parker's brain like gravel in a tin cup. "Carbon dioxide," he said. "That's it! That has to be it—it's a gas. You pump it into the ground to store it."

"You reduce carbon dioxide in the atmosphere by storing it underground," Relic agreed, "to help mitigate climate change."

"And it's leaking!" Parker shouted.

"That explains the low pressure they're worried about," Relic nodded.

"The low pressure readings prove that the gas is leaking out of the ground. There's a leak in the pipes. Or the geologic formation isn't a closed system." Parker slapped the papers with his hand.

"Not under pressure, at least."

"They're pushing carbon dioxide into the atmosphere instead of out of it," Parker said.

"That's how you suffocate in the open air. You breathe carbon dioxide instead of oxygen," Relic nodded.

"That gas is what's killing things," Parker said. "When they're low to the ground, near a leak."

"Bees and crows," Relic said.

"And humans?" Parker touched his breast.

CHAPTER 49

Dawson's pulse bucked against his chest and his veins squeezed into pinholes, explosive pressure building within the walls of his heart. The cat's keen eyes gleamed dark and deadly, glassy as wet opal.

He struck the match and held it into the grass and bark at the center of the stack of wood, blowing carefully, desperate to keep the flame alive. He glanced nervously at the crouching cougar, willing it to stop and reconsider.

He moved a twig into the fire and suddenly it dazzled, light licking against the rock shelter and out into the open.

Those jade eyes seemed to blink and, in the second it took Dawson to realize it, the cat had scurried into the night.

He took a long, deep breath.

Should he have tried to shoot it? Could he have aimed fast enough? If he'd missed, he'd have a wounded animal tearing into him with unbridled fury. Maybe he should fire a warning shot now to scare it farther away. But if he did, would the gunman hear it?

He settled on keeping the fire constant, its warmth a comfort to him. He didn't have that much firewood, so he'd have to feed it slowly over the course of the night and hope the lion would leave him alone. Maybe the smoke itself would help keep her at bay.

He thought of Sheriff Leavitt, Deputy Rowe, and Grace. Surely, they'd know he was in trouble by morning. If he could last that long.

Adrenaline suddenly depleted, his muscles felt weak and mushy. The flames danced before his eyes, swaying back and forth, out and in, rising and dropping hypnotically. He fought to stay awake, but he knew that fatigue, blood loss, and dehydration were taking their toll.

When he awoke, the fire had turned to hot ash. He quickly rebuilt it, laying the biggest piece of wood he had into the center, rejuvenating the flame.

Then he fell asleep again, snoring into the quiet of the night.

CHAPTER 50

Betty rubbed her eyes and sipped her latté. She'd had a terrible night, rolling in the bed until her sheet was wrapped twice around her legs, both of her arms hanging over the mattress. The thought of Cindy and Charles buying "tickets" together had her mind racing toward all kinds of disastrous conclusions. She resolved to stop her runaway thoughts, but the only thing that let her get any sleep at all was her decision to investigate first thing this morning.

The law firm booked all their travel through MTG, March Travel Guides, because they were inexpensive and good at finding package deals that combined hotels, airfare, and car rentals. But when the partners wanted a getaway, usually a side trip, they used their own personal accounts with a different travel agent. She'd booked her and Charles's airfare through an online company that way, to keep it private. But she knew that for at least one personal trip a few years ago, Charles had used Venture Travels, another agency in town. She decided to start there. She called the owner of Venture directly, a woman she'd worked with before, willing herself to stay calm and unrushed.

"Gene, this is Betty at Sapphire Solutions."

"Betty, how are you?

"Good, thanks, but we have a minor issue here with a couple of airline tickets. I'm hoping you can help us."

"Of course. Let me type in the name of your staff as it would appear on the tickets."

"Cindy Reid." Betty spelled the last name. "It seems she booked them this week, but she was in a car accident last night, and we have to cancel."

"Oh, dear, I hope she's alright."

"Well, we don't actually know yet. She was hit in the rear and is in pretty serious condition right now. We're hoping for a full recovery, but she'll be hospitalized for several days, according to her doctors."

"That's terrible."

"I know. And I'm not sure the details on that ticket…"

"That's all right. I see two tickets right here on my monitor."

Betty's fingers tightened against the phone.

"Let's see…They're fully refundable, but she booked them on a personal account."

"That's fine, just get the refund to whatever account she used."

"Sure. And…yes, they're booked for tomorrow morning, here to Denver, layover in Dallas, then to Belize."

The blood drained from Betty's cheeks.

"Odd. They're one-way tickets."

Betty cleared her throat. "That's understandable. We've got a client in Belize and sometimes it's easier to book one way there and book again when they know they are ready to come home."

"Nice to add a day or two down there, too, after business is done, huh? Enjoy the beaches, right?"

"Right. Did she book a ticket for Charles Story, too?"

"Yes. Same itinerary. Flight leaves tomorrow at ten-twelve in the morning."

One full day earlier than the tickets she had with Charles. "Thanks," Betty started to put the phone on her desk, her fingers numb.

"You want me to cancel both?"

"Oh, yes, thanks. Mr. Story canceled the meeting down there, after the accident. They'll make other arrangements later."

"All set. You want confirmation sent to you? Since Cindy is in the hospital?"

"Oh, yes, please." She gave Gene her personal email address, thanked her, and hung up.

She stared at her coffee, steam rising through the vent in the plastic lid. Then she reached behind her back, wound up her arm, and blasted the hot drink across her desk and into the wall on the other side of the room, dark liquid streaming down her Manager of the Year award.

CHAPTER 51

Parker rubbed the sleep from his eyes and sat up. Every muscle in his body ached and his shoulder hurt like needles had been driven into it. He took a long drink of water and discovered he was getting used to the taste. Well, a little bit. Relic was gone, his pack resting by the fire ring, the ashes cool as the morning air.

He rolled his arms and clenched his fists, working to warm up. He rewrapped the poncho over his shoulders and stared beyond their ledge to the river and cliffs beyond. Mounds of scree, tall as four-story buildings, accumulated below the high bluffs, rocks and sand eroded from above and deposited into wide piles that spread like fans down to the river bottom. The whole landscape was immense—solid earth hundreds of feet above the brown water, ridges upon ridges glowing into the distance.

Something seemed odd about one of the mounds across the river. Parker looked more closely. The rocks themselves appeared to move, rising and floating across the rugged landscape beneath them, and he was sure his eyes were playing tricks on him until he realized they were mountain sheep, tiny puffs of dust sprouting with each step.

Relic returned and began packing their gear. Parker scattered the fire rocks around the camp and buried the ash under fresh sand. They each had a sturdy piece of jerky to chew on. Parker carried the water bottle Relic had loaned him and they returned to the trail that would lead them to the top.

Within minutes, Parker began to sweat so he shed the poncho and tucked it under his arm. Relic's pace seemed almost leisurely. Did he ever tire out?

Eventually, the path twisted to the right and began to level. They crested a rise and the mesa spread before them like life on another planet. It had rained up here during the night, leaving pools and rivulets of water webbed across the rugged plain. The landscape appeared as one colossal, wrinkled hand, earthy capillaries flowing around fingers of barren sandstone.

He thought about what Relic had said, that we're all creatures of this magnificent place. The simple fact that we are here means that we belong, the society or politics or hatred of others be damned. How could he feel lonely in a place like this? He knelt and touched the cool sand at his feet and rested.

Relic must have sensed that he'd stopped. Relic set his pack on the ground and stretched.

They resumed their hike toward the east, the morning sun glaring into their eyes until it rose higher in the sky. Black figures floated in the air above them, circling the ground.

"Buzzards." Relic pointed. He led them closer, beneath their soaring wings.

The smell of a bloody carcass stung Parker's nose.

Relic searched the ground, nodded at something, and led them away. They walked across the mesa for what seemed like hours, up, down, over, and around an occasional patch of cacti or juniper.

Relic stopped suddenly, motioning for Parker to do the same. They'd come upon a rocky shelter, but Relic must have seen something he didn't like.

Relic slowly laid his pack on the ground and removed a metal contraption with something hanging from it. A slingshot. He collected several stones and crept quietly toward the outcrop. Then he armed the slingshot and fired it into the brush, yelling, shooting another stone, then another, stomping forward.

What was he doing?

A cougar half the size of an African lioness leapt from the brush a few yards away, its ears back in angry warning, hissing like a hot air balloon with a deadly leak.

Parker's chest tensed, lungs pasty, and he dropped his water bottle to the ground. He couldn't take his eyes off the wrathful cat.

Relic held his ground, firing another rock at the cougar, missing this time, but shooting again, making the animal step back.

Suddenly, the cat turned and trotted away, disappearing into a fold in the plateau like it had not a worry in the world.

Relic put his slingshot away and reshouldered his pack.

"What the hell?" Parker hurried to Relic.

"That lion was stalking something here." Relic pointed toward the rocks.

"I had no idea there were lions out here." Parker heard the quiver in his own voice.

"They're extremely shy of humans and their territory is huge. It's rare to ever see one."

Cold comfort in this instance, Parker thought.

"But this one's been hanging around the area. That carcass we passed a while back was a dead cougar cub. It might be hers; it might be keeping her close by. Or maybe something up ahead has been hurt. That cat can smell fresh blood from miles away."

They walked around to an opening in the ground. There, beneath an overhang, lay a man in a sheriff's uniform, one leg wrapped and bloody, his shoulders resting on the back of the shelter. He held a pistol on his lap, but his eyes were closed.

Relic and Parker looked at each other.

Relic walked slowly closer, speaking as he went. "Hey, are you all right?"

The lawman opened his eyes and raised his pistol. "Hold it right there."

CHAPTER 52

Betty wanted to march right up to Charles's office and shoot him in the face. Then his chest. Then his groin. Then his head again.

She'd shoot Cindy, too, that smug little nose blown back into her skull. Then her chest. Then her groin. Then her head again.

Damn it.

She didn't have a gun in her desk. She'd have to go home and get her .38 from her bedroom, pack some extra bullets, and get back to the office.

She took a long, deep breath and stared at the blank ceiling, clasping her hands together as if searching for some kind of transcendental intervention. She'd settle for psychic inspiration, but it didn't arrive.

She finally abandoned the idea of shooting their brains out. But the imagery was highly rewarding.

She could use a stiff drink about now, a margarita

with double the tequila, but she kept no alcohol at the office, either.

What was she going to do?

Everything was in place for the transfer of funds, the embezzlement of fifty-five million dollars. It had some complexities that could not be re-wired on short notice. The money would flow to the holding company, which had sham contracts in place with a dozen shell companies controlled by Mr. Smith. He would take ten percent of each amount transferred to each company and deposit the rest into corporate accounts in the Cayman Islands. Charles had fostered some very useful connections. Being a highly prized criminal defense attorney had its perks.

Betty was going to do the transfer of funds, but, really, Charles could do it just as easily. Without her.

She and Charles would receive their new identities and new passports in Belize in the names of the owners of those shell corporations. That would allow them to empty those funds into a personal account controlled only by her and Charles.

They would travel to Venezuela, where Mr. Smith had arranged a contact person for them there. They already had a house picked out, a beautiful home on a hill above the beach.

Smith's fee would be five-point-five million. The home in Venezuela would be paid in cash to one of the cartels that had used it in the past as a kind of safe house. There were some other fees to be paid under the table, too, but she and Charles would net about forty-five million dollars.

Some of that would buy a vacation home across the sea in Aruba and annual excursions throughout Europe. They planned to stay in Venezuela for only twelve months.

Charles's double-cross ignited her anger again, her cheeks flushing.

Mr. Smith was in on it too. He had to be. Which meant she couldn't go to Smith for a solution to her problem. She couldn't trust any of them.

Chances were, Charles had simply moved up the operation by one day and substituted Cindy for her. It was too complicated to change anything else.

That had to be it, she thought. A simple substitution of consorts and the money transfers to occur one day early.

How could she stop his plan and still keep the money for herself?

CHAPTER 53

"I never learn," Relic mumbled and raised his arms in the air. "No good deed goes unpunished."

Parker raised his arms, too, and stared at the man on the ground. "What are you doing here?"

The lawman's pistol drooped in his fingers and slowly lowered to his waist. His eyes closed and he moved his mouth, but no sound came out. They waited and watched him for a minute before Parker decided to take a chance. Arms still in the air, he took one step after another toward the lawman.

"He's wounded." Relic pointed at him and moved closer. "And exhausted."

They lowered their hands and knelt next to him. Relic pulled the pistol from his fingers and set it aside.

"You are both under arrest," the man said, voice dry as gravel.

Relic squeezed the man's lips open and dribbled

water over them. The lawman reacted a moment later, taking the liquid into his mouth, swallowing in feeble sips. Relic stopped and let him catch his breath, then repeated the process, getting as much water into him as he could.

Parker and Relic sat on either side of the man, a patch on his chest identifying him as a deputy sheriff. He opened his eyes and stared past them, out into the plateau. Relic offered him water again, drawing his attention slowly back.

The deputy took a long, lustful drink of water, nearly a quarter of Relic's bottle. He wiped his lips and nodded. "Thank you."

"Did you see that cougar?" Parker pointed outside the shelter. "It was stalking you."

"Yeah. Last night, I realized what it was." He swallowed. "Fire kept it away."

"For a while," Parker said. "It was creeping up on you just now. Relic hit it with a sling shot and scared it off."

The deputy looked at Relic, then Parker, then back at Relic. "Who the hell are you guys?"

They introduced themselves. "You," Dawson pointed to Relic. Dawson's eyelids fluttered, the man close to passing out again, but then he recovered, his jaw tightened, and he said, "You are under arrest."

Relic rolled his eyes.

"What?" Parker said.

"What do you know about a dead man in the can-yon?" Dawson pushed his words at Relic. "By the Cedar Flute ruins."

"Not much. Found him dead a few days ago, along with a bunch of bees and a crow. Saw a dead cougar cub on our way here."

Dawson stared at Relic. "Found him?"

"Right."

"You didn't choke him to death?"

"What?" Parker said again.

"Would I be here right now, helping you, if I had killed that man?" Relic set his water bottle next to Dawson, stood, and walked away.

"You're an idiot," Parker told Dawson.

"Just doing my job. I have to ask."

Parker stood. "That man just saved your life."

"Did you see the professor too?" he asked Parker.

"Professor?"

"The dead man was a professor."

"No."

"What are you doing out here?"

"Long story." Parker turned to leave.

"Wait, wait," Dawson pawed the dirt with his hand. "I'm sorry, I'm not thinking straight…"

"I'll say."

"I'm here investigating the death of the professor and looking for your friend there. In fact," he took a breath, "I think I've been looking for him for a long time now."

"Well, we found you, sheriff."

"Deputy."

Parker checked that Dawson's gun was beyond his reach.

"I'm sorry. I made a mistake. Please, I just want to ask you guys some questions."

"You need medical help." Parker nodded toward the blood on Dawson's thigh.

"I need to get back to my Jeep. Back to the pumping station."

Parker's breath caught in his throat. "Did you say… you came from the pumping station?"

CHAPTER 54

Betty locked the door to her office and paced the room. Charles's plan had been simple. Hers had to be just as short and sweet, direct, and unavoidable.

She stopped and stared at an empty wall. She tugged a pencil width of hair into her mouth and chewed on it.

Substitution. That was what Charles had done and that was what she could do, only in reverse. If Cindy was out of the picture, what would happen? Charles couldn't leave with Cindy one day earlier than he had originally planned. There would be no time to change arrangements for the transfer of funds. He'd have to play along with her and leave the following day, the day she and Charles had planned from the beginning. All of the original plan would remain in place if Cindy were eliminated.

Would Charles suspect anything? Maybe. But he couldn't confront her without admitting the plan to double-cross her. He was a sneaky, low-down, conniving bastard, but he was too greedy to turn away from what had taken two years for them to put together. If Cindy were eliminated, Charles would stick with the original plan and the two of them would be in Belize, then Aruba, within the week.

Charles would have to go with his plan B. Her plan A.

After that, she would find a way to eliminate Charles. Maybe at the old safe house in Venezuela. An unfortunate boating accident. A drowning. A disappearance in the Bermuda Triangle.

After that, she could sell the house and find a villa on the Tunisian coast, where there was no extradition treaty with the United States. And she could do it all on her own.

No more Charles. No more Cindy.

How best to eliminate Cindy? It had to be simple, too, and nothing too suspicious. Nothing to interest law enforcement.

She knew she couldn't trust Mr. Smith anymore.

But she had just the thing.

CHAPTER 55

"Why were you at the pumping station?" Parker asked Dawson.

"Investigating the death of the professor. Down by the ruins."

Relic came back toward Dawson. "Why are they connected?"

Dawson looked at him, suspicion in his tired eyes. "Because the man who killed him, or maybe the man who found him, ran up to the top of this mesa. He got up the slot canyon somehow. I drove up here to see if I could circle around and find him." He examined Relic like a cut of steak. "And I did find him."

"I'm the connection?" Relic said.

"But why are you bleeding? Why are you hurt?" Parker asked.

"You..." Dawson pointed a finger at Relic, "...are under arrest."

Parker spoke more forcefully. "How did you get hurt?"

Dawson turned away from Relic. "Your name is Parker." They'd introduced themselves a few minutes earlier, but Dawson announced it like a fact he'd just confirmed.

"Yes."

"You are hereby deputized." Dawson waved his hand at him.

"Thank you," Parker said, exchanging a meaningful glance with Relic. "But why are you hurt?"

"Arrest that man." Dawson pointed at Relic again.

"He's feverish," Relic spoke under his breath.

"Sure, sure." Parker drew Dawson's attention back to him. "But what happened to your leg?"

"Shot, it was." Dawson's eyes flipped into the back of his head for a second then rolled forward again.

Relic whispered, "Ask him how the man at the ruins was killed."

Parker asked.

"Suffocated. Right there out in the open, lips as blue as...." Dawson's voice trailed away.

"That's right. The dead man," Relic's eyes flashed. "The professor. His lips were indeed blue. The carbon dioxide your bosses are pumping into the ground is leaking out and it killed him, the bees, the crow, the cougar cub…"

Dawson looked from Relic to Parker and back again, confusion on his face.

"The guy who shot me…" Parker rubbed the bandage on his shoulder. "His pals must still be up here, Relic."

"Who?" Dawson asked.

"And they got the drop on the sheriff, here," Relic said.

"Deputy," Dawson corrected.

"I guess so," Parker examined the bloody T-shirt wrapped on Dawson's leg.

"He's not in any condition to move." Relic pointed at the deputy.

"You're under arrest," Dawson said to Relic again.

"We'll have to bring help to him." Parker nodded.

"Which means we still have to get to the pump station so you can call for help. There must be a radio—the deputy must have driven a vehicle to get here," Relic said. "Should we get his keys?"

"Sure." Parker shook Dawson's shoulder to help him focus. "I'm going to need your car keys," Parker motioned his chin toward Relic, "so I can arrest that man."

Dawson seemed to consider the request.

"Your car keys?" Parker repeated.

Dawson nodded and pulled them from his front pants pocket. Parker lifted the key ring from the deputy's fingers.

Parker turned and whispered to Relic, "Gun?"

Relic nodded.

"I need your gun for a while, too." Parker turned back to Dawson. "For the arrest…" He slid it farther from Dawson's hand and picked it up.

Parker and Relic took a step back from him.

"Should we keep the gun?" Parker asked.

"Yeah. I think we've chased that cat away for good. And if he tried to shoot it, he's just as likely to shoot himself," Relic said.

"Deputy, arrest that man," Dawson ordered again, his eyes flashing wide but unfocused. As the last word left his lips, he collapsed into unconsciousness.

"We're going to have to move quickly," Relic said.

"Leave him some water?" Parker asked.

"And the M&M's."

CHAPTER 56

Betty checked the office calendar on her computer screen. Charles had a two o'clock appointment out of the office, so she planned to go up there shortly. She placed a small, over-the-counter item from the pharmacy into her pants pocket and checked her lipstick and hair.

Her heels clacked against the terrazzo floor of the main lobby and she nodded at Rodney, the security guard, as she walked by. Across the street, she ordered two caramel lattés, paid in cash, and returned to the office building. The elevator was empty, so she rode to the fourth floor alone. On the way, she put five drops of something into the latté marked "Charles."

She leaned into the glass door that led to the law offices and slid into the hallway. The conference room on her left was full of people—clients, attorneys from the firm, and opposing counsel. She could guess which ones the clients were—their foreheads creased, fists clenched. Some kind of negotiation, she assumed, civilized but intense.

Cindy sat at her desk at the end of the hall, just outside the corner office that Charles used. Her eyes were on her computer screen, but she seemed unfocused. Looking forward to that trip to Belize tomorrow with her boyfriend, Betty mused.

She put on her best smile and strode up to Cindy's desk. "Is Charles in?"

Cindy turned to greet her. "No, he's out with a client."

"Oh, shoot," Betty pouted. "I forgot to check the office calendar."

"He won't be back until about three o'clock."

"Well…" She pretended to think. "If he's not going to enjoy a fresh latté, then you may as well drink it while it's hot."

"Flavored?" Cindy asked, a hint of anticipation in her voice.

"Of course." Betty handed her the cup. "Caramel."

"Oh, my favorite."

"Mine, too."

Cindy took a small sip of the drink.

Betty removed the lid from hers and blew on the liquid to cool it. "This steamed milk is the best."

"Mmm." Cindy took a swallow.

"How have things been going for you?" Betty snapped the lid back in place.

"Oh," Cindy shrugged her shoulders.

Did she just blush? Betty knew she had and knew exactly why, but she put her lips to the coffee and focused on the floor.

"Yeah, things are good." Cindy had recovered. "Busy, but not too hectic, you know?"

"Yes, that's great. Charles's one of the best lawyers to work for around here." Betty took a noisy sip. She'd seen enough. Cindy would drink most, if not all, of the latté Betty had supposedly brought for Charles. She would feel some disorientation first, then blurred vision and difficulty breathing. Her lips and fingernails would begin to turn bluish—she'd know something was wrong as the symptoms slowly washed over her. She could become deathly ill by the end of the day, maybe even hospitalized by tonight, but Betty had tried not to overdo it. She wasn't worried that she might have put too much poison in the cup—it was no skin off her teeth, as they say. But she only needed the woman out of the picture tomorrow and the next day.

"Yes." Cindy nodded.

"Well, enjoy the coffee." Betty waved her hand at

Cindy and turned to walk away.

She'd return to Cindy's desk after the office had closed for the day and make sure to dispose of the poison in her pocket and the coffee cup. She'd thought of a trash bin two blocks away, behind a little café, where they would be carried away to the dump and disappear for good.

CHAPTER 57

Relic and Parker walked side-by-side across the plateau, weaving between the sage and occasional thickets of prickly pear cacti, quiet in thought. They climbed a gentle rise in the landscape and continued north and east another four miles before Relic had them stop for water and protein bars. Parker knew what they needed to do, but he had no idea how.

Relic pulled binoculars from a pocket in his pants and crawled to a rise in front of them. He watched for a while then motioned for Parker to come and see too.

The pump station lay gray in the haze. Behind it sat the trailer house. To the right of the pumps were Dom's old Bronco, the blackened hulk of a truck, and a dark suburban. The SUV was new. Behind and to the right of them, a bit up the dirt road, was a Jeep with a county sheriff icon on the side door and a high antenna arched over the roofline. He couldn't see any people around—

no movement, no puffs of dust, nothing.

The hollow-faced man and his partner had driven Parker and Dom in the black pickup truck, which Relic had burned. The partner had gone over the cliff with Dom. The presence of the SUV meant that Wicks had called for help, a replacement for his original partner.

Not good.

Had he gotten only one replacement? Or several?

Rain had blessed the ground up here late last night or early this morning. The glare of standing water surrounded the pumps and pooled in places along the old road. He scanned the area close to where they lay, then farther out toward the trailer house.

"See anyone?"

"No." He handed the binoculars back to Relic.

"Me neither."

"They should be searching for us."

Relic huffed. "They didn't strike me as the hiking type."

"Are they waiting for us to come to them?"

Relic ran his fingers through his goatee. "Maybe. They did send that guy down the far canyon, which means he walked back up the road a ways, to a place where you can get into it. The canyon starts as a shallow arroyo up that way." He pointed to the east.

"That's the guy who almost caught us in the ruins."

Relic nodded. "There's only two easy ways for him to leave the ruins, so he'd either be walking the road that starts there, a long way back to the highway, or he's retracing his steps and coming back up through the canyon. Which would bring him back somewhere to the right of the pump station."

"It'll take him all day to get back here, if that's what he's doing, you think?"

"Yeah, at least. I think he's not back here yet. Maybe the guys in the trailer are waiting for him."

"Or for us," Parker whispered.

"Watch for an old-fashioned ambush."

"But we've got to get to the deputy's Jeep to call for help."

"Let's work our way to the pumps. They'll hide our approach, at least as we get closer," Relic said.

"You think they're in the trailer?"

"In it or near it. Or maybe in their car."

"What then? Make a run for the Jeep?"

"We go slow until we can't anymore. If they see us, we run like hell for the Jeep."

Parker's stomach knotted into a ball.

CHAPTER 58

"Here." Parker handed Dawson's pistol to Relic, butt first. "You might know more about how to use this than me."

"Yep." He slipped it under his belt. "Let's split up in case they start shooting at us. Two targets are harder to hit than one."

Parker wiped the sweat from his forehead. He returned the binoculars to Relic, who tucked them into his pocket.

"You have the deputy's keys," Relic said, "so you can head pretty much straight for the Jeep to call for help. You'll have a couple places to hide behind on the way. That corner of the pump station," he pointed, "and that utility pole there. It looks like an electric box on the side, about waist high. There's also a red tank farther right, above the ground, on metal braces. Probably a fuel tank. The SUV is beyond the tank, between the electric pole and the Jeep. You can get behind it as you make your way there."

"Where will you be?"

"I'll go left to the southwestern edge of the pumps. I'll cover your approach, and if we see anybody, I'll create a diversion. If I fire the pistol, they'll come after me as you go for the Jeep."

"Sounds risky."

"Yep."

"And we don't know how many of them there are."

"Yep."

"But Dawson is not going to survive if we hike the long way out of here."

"Yep. We're talking two full days, maybe a little more."

"Well…"

"If we run into them, I'll lead them away. I can lose 'em or outrun 'em over open ground. If I break free of them, I'll get back to Dawson and see if I can get him to drink more water."

"Right."

"How's your shoulder feelin'?"

"A little stiff but not too bad."

"Good. After you call for help, just stay where you are. Or, if it's safe, you could even take off in the sheriff's Jeep. Take the dirt road to the highway and turn right and you'll head into town."

Parker's intestines twisted on themselves. "Right."

"I'll get back to Dawson and see if I can help the paramedics find him."

"Good idea."

"Any last minute questions?"

"Got any more stupid jokes?"

Relic shook his head. "Nah…it's your turn."

Parker looked toward the pumps and the SUV. "No jokes, just a question. Are we about to have one of those human experiences you mentioned?"

Relic's white teeth gleamed.

CHAPTER 59

Relic trotted toward the left side of the pumps, still about a mile away.

Rain streaked from pewter-colored clouds in the east, paints brushed downward across the afternoon canvas. Moist sage spiced the air, their leaves cupping shallow drops, funneling them to their roots. Pools formed in low spots across the mesa, but the spaces in between had already dried in the desert air. Parker wished it were raining now, to keep the gunmen hunkered down.

Parker hiked forward, aiming for the electric pole on the right side of the pumps. At first, he walked erect, watching for any signs of movement by the trailer or vehicles. The ground rose and fell unevenly at times, but he eventually came to a small rise and decided to bend lower to the ground. He dropped his eyes to his feet so as not to trip and kept the utility pole between himself and the trailer. A gust of wind rose behind him and pushed his clothing tight against his skin. Moments later, it rocked the metal trailer, and he thought it would either grab the attention of those inside or keep them sheltered there.

He glanced to his left, where Relic continued to jog toward the far end of the pumps.

The utility pole grew larger in his view until finally he was only a few yards away. Relic had reached the pumps on the opposite corner.

Bang!

A metal door slammed open, tossed by the wind. A blond man with a sidearm in his holster stepped out of the trailer and wrestled the door behind him, finally getting it closed. He had to be someone the hollow-faced man had called in to help.

The wind stopped as suddenly as it had hit.

Parker ducked down, putting the electric box between him and the gunman. He moved closer to the utilities, squatting as he walked to the base of the wooden pole.

The blond checked his pistol, his face examining the clip as he pulled it out and snapped it back into place. He stepped down to the ground and began to walk toward the SUV, checking inside and underneath. He moved away then did a visual search of the whole area, slowly rotating on his heels. Satisfied, he began walking directly toward the electric pole and where Parker was hiding.

Shit.

The electric box hung a couple of feet above a concrete pad that had collected rainwater, its door ajar.

A separate system led from the elevated fuel tank and tractor-sized engine to another junction box a few yards away. A back-up system if the electric grid ever failed.

The concrete pad supported each of the pumps. Six rows paralleled each other between him and Relic, aisles running crossways between them. They were both at the back of the rows, the side farthest from the trailer house. If Relic or Parker stepped into a row, neither would be able to see the other.

If Parker could get to the nearest row, he could hide on the end and duck away as the gunman approached. But he'd have to get from the power pole to that first row. Then, if he stayed ahead of the gunman, he might be able to circle behind him, safe in a place the man had already searched.

He readied himself to sprint to the first row of pumps.

The blond stopped and looked toward the trailer, where another gunman had walked outside.

The blond man motioned to the other.

They were lining up so that each took one aisle through the pumps simultaneously, the nearest man— the blond—taking the row between the last pump and the electric box. He resumed his walk, heading directly for Parker.

CHAPTER 60

Betty checked the clock on the wall: nearly four-forty. The office calendar put Charles in a meeting in the conference room until five, so she'd come upstairs to see if he might be finished. This was going to be a challenge for her. As angry and hurt and thoroughly pissed as she was, she was going to have to act like nothing was wrong. Like their plan had never varied and she was still excited to run away with him to Belize the day after tomorrow. If she could stay focused on what she'd dreamed about for so long, the money, the beaches, and the travels through Europe, she could pull it off.

Two gray-haired women left the large room together, looking tired. Betty nodded to them as they passed and glanced inside. Charles was there by himself, tucking papers into his briefcase.

She took a breath and went inside.

"How are things?" She smiled her best smile at

him, projecting warmth and optimism.

He looked up from his papers, tiny circles under his eyes, his skin as pale as an eggshell. He seemed a little startled but recovered quickly. "Long day."

"Yes, but…" She looked about the empty room surreptitiously, a sly grin on her lips. "Day after tomorrow, we'll be on a sunny beach sipping margaritas."

"Indeed." He closed his briefcase.

"So, cheer up, sweetheart, we're nearly there." She ran a finger across the table suggestively.

"Yes, well, slight hiccup," he began, his Adam's apple bobbing in his throat.

She raised her brow.

"Cindy left the office an hour ago, sick as a dog. Had to get paramedics to take her to the hospital."

"Oh, dear."

"Yeah, well, awkward timing…"

"I suppose." Betty circled her finger on the tabletop. "But you can type your own memos for a day or two and she's young. Probably a bad case of the flu that's going around."

"Yes." He nodded.

"Actually, the timing is perfect." She watched him under her brow, waiting to see what he thought she might mean.

"Oh?" He swallowed a mouthful of saliva as if it were broken glass.

"Well, dear, tomorrow you need to tell people that you're not feeling well so you can call in sick the day after. Maybe Cindy gave it to you. You're going to say it's Covid, remember?"

"Oh, yes, of course." He looked relieved.

Toying with him was turning out to be rather fun.

"I can't wait to get you in the hotel room in Belize," she whispered.

He straightened his back. "Betty, we can't possibly talk like that here."

She glanced at the empty hall outside the room. "I know. I just can't wait to get you there." She batted her eyelashes once and turned to leave.

CHAPTER 61

Relic was forty yards away, on the other side of the pump station. The gunman walking toward Parker was beyond Relic's line of sight. Parker pointed a finger toward the man, moving it so Relic could see it, but the gunman could not. Relic raised a hand, recognizing Parker's signal.

The man would be on top of Parker at any moment.

He squeezed more tightly against the utility pole, knowing he'd soon be discovered, knowing he had no time and no place to run. Fear coursed through his blood, panic surging over him. What could he do? What could he possibly do? He thought of Dom and his courage and the fact that he'd taken a bad man with him to the bottom of those cliffs. Parker wasn't going to take anyone with him, though. He didn't even have a rock to throw at the blond man—it would be bare fists against a pistol.

He'd never felt so helpless and utterly pathetic.

Pow!

The gunman ducked lower to the ground and turned away from Parker. He scurried to the pump on the corner of the concrete pad, shoes splashing in the puddles, and peered around it.

Relic had retreated from the pumps to a lump of rock in the ground but stood tall behind it, gun in the air.

"This is Sheriff Dawson!" Relic yelled.

For some dumb reason, Parker imagined Dawson correcting him: "Deputy—not sheriff." And who would believe that a ponytailed, tough-as-nails hermit was a law enforcement officer?

"Surrender your weapons and come out with your hands up."

Cliché, but Relic sounded like he meant it.

The blond gunman crouched low to the ground. Pow! He'd fired a shot at Relic, who dropped low to the rock.

Parker couldn't see the second gunman, but knew he must be focused on Relic too.

He scooted closer to the electrical box, wondering now whether he could escape to the Jeep up the road and call for help. Or whether he could sprint the distance to the nearest gunman and overpower him while Relic kept his attention.

Pow! Another shot from the blond. Parker saw a spit of dust rise near Relic's feet.

Pow! Pow! He could hear the other gunman firing at Relic from behind one of the pumps, about forty feet away. Parker saw Relic rise and fall flat again, a fresh swirl of red dust bursting from the ground.

All grew quiet except for the low hum of the electric pumps, a weird and disturbing vibration that penetrated his skull and numbed his eardrums.

All he could see of Relic was the hump of his daypack, but it was absolutely still.

The dust near Relic spread into the breeze.

He and the blond gunman watched intently for any movement. Had his bullets hit their mark? Had Relic been wounded? Or worse?

Pow! Pow! The blond fired two more rounds but still Relic did not move, did not react at all, and Parker flinched, the thought of losing another friend absolutely jarring. He turned his head toward the open utility box and stared at the gray container, hypnotized by the odd-looking thing and he seemed to really see it for the first time. Suddenly, he had an idea born of panic.

The door to the box hung open. Inside, heavy wire encased in white rubber ran down the pole, looped around itself, and into a junction. From there, wires ran back up the pole and crossed to the pumps.

The white, rubber-coated wire was live.

He yanked the wire from the junction box, unwinding the loops, then jammed it into a pool of water atop the concrete foundation. The hair on his head and neck lifted erect, his fingers tingled with tiny, shivering, electrons, and hot current ran though the wet and into the blond gunman kneeling at the corner. His body seized firm, his muscles tense, a weightlifter struggling for that final pull, his legs and arms straight and stiff, the gun flung from his hand. The man snorted and shivered in the roiling current and then collapsed, face down.

Parker lifted the wire from the water.

The man moaned but did not move.

The pumps whined like tired infants, slowly starved of energy, winding downward, finally falling asleep.

The quiet was a little unnerving.

He tucked the wire into a hinge in the junction box, leaving the bare end hanging loose, hoping it would stay safely in place, then he ran to the blond. He took a moment to look at him, watching for any movement. He listened for sounds from the other gunman but heard nothing.

Plastic zip ties were wound around the blond

man's belt, so Parker wrapped one around each of the guy's wrists. He pulled the wrists close together behind his back and attached them with a third tie. Then he did the same with the man's ankles.

Was the guy alive?

Parker held his hand under the man's nose and felt a subtle draw of air then realized he didn't really care whether the blond man lived or died, and the callous thought itself was of no concern to him.

He had to check on Relic.

CHAPTER 62

The sun angled through her office window, heating the air, relaxing her. She'd helped spread the word that Charles was feeling ill and helped him reschedule tomorrow's appointments. He'd be calling in sick, though he was actually fine. They had an afternoon flight together to Belize.

She and Charles had already transferred most of their money to accounts in Belize under new names and identities. Not that they'd need the money after she and Charles swept fifty-five million from the Solar Gem accounts later today.

After that, as the saying went, the world was their oyster.

Cindy remained in the intensive care unit, unconscious. The doctors hadn't yet figured out the cause of her condition and likely never would. Despite that, the doctors were optimistic, saying she'd probably have a full recovery. Then she could steal some other woman's man...

Of course, Charles had to go. She no longer trusted him to do anything beyond his own immediate, selfish interests. They needed each other at least until Venezuela. Smith had good contacts in the country, which is why they were going there. But she couldn't trust Smith anymore, either, so Venezuela also represented a danger. Betty would need to act quickly once they'd moved to the coastal villa there, northwest of Caracas.

She had just the plan: quick and deadly. Once Smith had been fully paid and Charles was gone, Smith wouldn't give a rat's ass about Betty or what she had done. She would never return to Caracas, though, or even to Belize, for that matter, and certainly not to the United States. Instead, she had plans to travel leisurely throughout Europe.

She was really going to enjoy being a widow.

CHAPTER 63

Parker hurried past the first row of pumps. He peeked around the corner. The second gunman lay crumpled on the concrete pad, knees tucked to his stomach. Parker walked carefully toward him.

A clunk and a whir made him jump and he searched the area for the source of the sounds. A large tractor-type engine beyond the utility pole had started running. Above it rose the red tank that must hold gasoline, fuel for an automated back-up generator.

He sighed and turned his attention back to the second gunman. The man seemed to be unconscious. Parker placed one tie on the man's left wrist and pulled it tight. He had to maneuver him to reach his right wrist, which was under his stomach. Parker laid the ties on the ground and pushed against the guy's shoulder, trying to roll him over, and just as he did, the man pulled away and raised a pistol at Parker's chest.

He stepped away from the gunman and blinked, the appearance of the pistol so fast and sudden, he had trouble registering the fact that it had happened. His muscles seemed to lose their elasticity, his breath frozen in his lungs.

Another pistol appeared in his periphery, Dawson's Glock, sliding closer to the gunman's head and, when the man looked up, Parker followed his gaze to Relic.

"No, no," Relic said quietly.

The gunman lowered his pistol to the concrete pad. He turned his head away from Parker and released a long huff of air. Parker shook himself into action and used the zip ties to finish the job, restraining the man's wrists and ankles.

"The other guy?" Relic asked.

"Tied up a few rows over."

"I'll take this one's car keys, just to be sure he stays put." Relic felt into the man's pockets and pulled out a cell phone.

"Hey, that's mine." Parker took it.

Relic rummaged again and pulled out a ring of keys and a black fob.

"We can take his SUV," Parker nodded, "to get out of here."

"Did you see any more of them?"

"No. Just these two."

"Well, and the one that chased us to the ruins," Relic said.

"True, but he's a long way from here."

"So were we, yesterday."

"Right."

"Let's step away." Relic lowered the Glock and they walked to the end of the row opposite the gunman, closer to the road and the abandoned trailer.

Parker rested his hands on his knees and tried to relax his breathing. "Thank god you're okay," he said.

"Well..." Relic pulled his pack from his back and wiggled a finger through a bullet hole. Parker could see three more of them, clean punctures in the fabric, their edges in circles and ellipses.

A burst of relief rushed through Parker, and he laughed.

They stood there for a while, Relic fiddling with the fresh holes in his pack, checking for damaged goods. Parker stood and stretched then rested his hand on one of the pipes on the pump station. The vibrations had resumed when the back-up generator kicked on. He looked to his left, where one of the new, blue-backed gauges read 2,100 psi.

"Hey. The pumps are on again and those messed

up gauges are on again, too—the ones Dom and I figured that Betty messed with. These guys," he waved toward the gunmen, "must have put them on."

"So they're reading as if they're normal, but they're not." Relic stared at the new instrument.

"They're pumping CO2 directly into the atmosphere." Parker pointed to the sky.

"Back to killing bees and crows and cougar cubs."

"And maybe humans," Parker said.

Relic's dark eyes narrowed into fissures in his weathered face.

CHAPTER 64

Relic reshouldered his pack and stomped toward the sheriff's Jeep.

Parker glanced at the gunman and decided he didn't want to be left alone with him, hobbled or not. He hurried after Relic.

They crossed the dirt road, dodging spots that were still wet from the rain. The Jeep looked well-used, with clumps of dried mud in the wheel wells and faded paint on the hood and roof. A long antenna anchored at the rear bumper arched over the top of the Jeep in a half-circle, connected on the other end below the windshield. A silver star, the seal of the sheriff, plastered the driver's side door.

He looked for the blond gunman along the rows of pumps and saw him squirming off the concrete pad and into the dust. He knew he couldn't walk or run but the sight of him still made Parker stiffen.

He ran the rest of the way to the Jeep, where Relic had opened the rear hatch.

"Try your phone." Relic rummaged through gear in the back of the Jeep.

"Right." Parker tried without success. There were no bars showing available service and the battery was nearly dead, anyway. He'd forgotten to charge it back at the office, before the hollow-faced man had first arrived. "Why don't I try the radio?"

"Good idea." Relic stuffed some things into a black duffle bag.

"What are you doing?" Parker asked.

"Taking this. It's an 'oh-shit bag' for emergencies. It's got water filters, first aid, food, matches, all kinds of survival gear."

"Taking it where?"

Relic turned to him. "You've been deputized, right?"

"What?"

"Deputy Dawson deputized you, right?"

"He's half out of his mind." Parker spread his arms.

"Which means the other half is fine."

"What are you thinking?"

"With your permission, deputy, I'm taking this duffle. I'll go back to Dawson and use the first aid kit. Like we said before, I'll see if I can help search and rescue find him."

"Okay."

"And I can leave him his gun."

"Sure. Then what?"

"You call for help on the radio. Tell them he's in bad shape. He needs an IV for fluids. Get a chopper to come, if you can."

"What about those guys?" He swept his hand toward the gunmen bound with zip ties.

"They're in a world of trouble," Relic said.

"As long as they don't find a way out of that trouble."

"Stupidity got them into this mess. I'd guess it's not going to get them out."

"You're coming back here, right?"

Relic pulled the duffle from the Jeep. "Nope. I'm going home. I'll stay with Dawson as long as I can help him, but then I'm out of here."

"Oh." He hadn't thought about parting from Relic. "I'll be here with these guys all by myself…"

"You can leave in the sheriff's Jeep. Better yet, leave in the Bronco…" Relic set the duffle on the ground and searched his pockets. "With this." He handed Parker a black wire with metal pieces on the ends. "I should've given it to you earlier."

"What is it?"

"Distributor wire. Raise the hood, put the wire back in place, and this thing will run fine. Just look for the two empty sockets on top of the engine and connect them. Keys are still in the ignition. You can get out of here after you call for help, if you want."

"What about the SUV?" Parker pointed at the shiny black tank. "You took the gunman's keys, remember?"

"I have other plans for that." Relic lifted the duffle and patted Parker on his arm. "Remember to do your best."

"Right…"

"And have some fun along the way."

"But…"

Relic glanced around then began a steady trot toward the SUV.

CHAPTER 65

Parker hustled to the driver's side of the Jeep and looked through the cab. He had the deputy's keys in his pocket.

Relic was gone. Was he going to drive the SUV across the mesa?

The radio seemed straightforward enough—volume knob on the left, digital read out in the center, frequency arrows on the right. He climbed inside and turned on the battery power. Little red lights glowed on the radio, displaying a frequency he assumed was for the sheriff's office.

He pulled the microphone from its cradle and pushed the button to speak. What should he say?

"Mayday, mayday, is anyone out there?" The radio squealed when he released the microphone button. He repeated the call four times. Finally, a sound like rustling paper came across the speaker.

"Sherriff's office, Grace here. Who is on this

frequency?"

"Oh, thank god." Parker's shoulders relaxed and he spoke into the microphone again, telling Grace who he was and that medics were needed as soon as possible for Dawson—he'd been shot and was losing blood. Get a helicopter if they have one.

Grace's voice dimmed, her concern obvious even over the airwaves. She promised help right away. GPS showed the Jeep at the pump station, but where, exactly, was Dawson?

"The deputy is south of here. There should be a little smoke where he's camped, several miles from…"

Boots scraped across the ground outside the Jeep. Parker turned his head back and forth, searching for the source. Had Relic returned? Had one of the gunmen managed to walk over here? He swiveled his head all around but saw nothing.

"Are you still there? Can you still hear me?" Grace asked. "There's something…"

Hollow-faced man rose slowly from the front of the Jeep, cavernous eyes storms of pent-up anger. His forehead was sunburned, his sweater roughed from wear, twigs stuck haphazardly into the weave. His hair had matted to his scalp like he'd poured cooking grease over the top of his head.

They stared at each other, steeled in the moment, then Parker dropped the microphone to the floor. The hollow-faced man rubbed his hands together, a praying mantis eager for its meal.

Parker reached for the door to pull it shut but the man was faster, rounding the side and grabbing the handle before it closed. He yanked the door from Parker's hand and reached for his ankle. Parker kicked and kicked, but the gunman had a firm grip and pulled him across the seat of the Jeep. Parker grabbed the steering wheel and held tight. The hollow-faced man had him stretched out the open door, only his head and arms inside. The pull sent a piercing pain through the wound in his shoulder and his left hand lost its grip. Another yank dragged him out of the vehicle, slamming his head against the edge of the door and onto the ground.

The man lifted Parker by his shirt and pounded a fist into the side of his face, splitting his lip, hurling him back into the dirt. The sky seemed to spin above him, and his head ached with the pounding hooves of fleeing horses.

CHAPTER 66

Parker's vision blurred, then slowly cleared. The hollow-faced man stood above him, hands on his hips, panting. Their struggle had taken a toll on him, too, but he was clearly in control.

Parker could see the SUV behind the man, several yards away. Where the hell was Relic?

The man stepped closer to Parker and began to lean in for another strike. Parker crawled backward toward the Jeep, his left shoulder stiff with pain, his shirt wet with fresh blood. The wound had re-opened.

The man took another step toward him, fists in the air.

Parker raised his knees, pulling his feet beneath them, and pushed away again. He scrambled with his hands behind his head, a sprawling, awkward backstroke across solid ground.

The man's lips pressed into a narrow line above his

chin, determined to beat Parker again.

Something shifted in Parker's chest, fear now turned to rage as he'd had enough of this man who dared to strike him a second time, indeed, who dared again to try to kill him. A favorite photo of his sister flashed in his head, and he thought about how drugs had put her to sleep forever young and how these thugs had knocked him out and had come up here to kill him and Dom. All to hide a lousy theft. All to hide a gas spewed by the broken pumping station from hell. All these thoughts formed in the same split second it took for his heart to pound a single beat. He'd never been so angry in his life.

Parker scoured the dirt around him and found a stone the size of a small orange. He wrapped his fingers around it and, as the hollow-faced man reached for Parker's shirt again, he swung it hard against the man's wrist. The man yelped and stepped away, cradling his hand.

Parker lifted himself against the front of the Jeep, keeping his injured side away from the man, and charged him, swinging his rock again.

The man stepped away easily and Parker spun past him and turned around.

Parker moved forward, rock raised for another blow, but the man circled, putting Parker's back against the Jeep again. Just as Parker readied to attack once more, the man reached beneath his sweater, pulled a silver Glock 17, and pointed it at Parker's head.

He stopped in his tracks.

They both heard the black SUV start and rev its engine.

The hollow-faced man, fully confident now, stepped away to look at the SUV.

Parker pulled his shoulder back and threw the rock as hard as he could, like a baseball, and it struck the back of the man's head with a crack. The man's knees folded downward and he rolled to the ground and onto his back, his arms spread across the dusty road.

Relic drove the SUV backward along the ground, slowly distancing from the pump station. What the hell was he doing?

Parker ran to the hollow-faced man and took the gun from his fingers. He moved away from the man's reach, keeping the pistol aimed at his chest.

He looked all around him now, searching for anyone else he should worry about.

The SUV disappeared behind a low hill.

In the opposite direction, far along the dirt road and away from the station, rose a rooster tail of dust.

Another vehicle was moving this way, and fast.

CHAPTER 67

The sheriff couldn't have gotten help here this quickly, could he? Parker stared at the moving dot, willing it to be help and not more reinforcements for the gunmen. He couldn't take any more fighting.

The hollow-faced man groaned, gathering his reserve, pulling his arms to his head. He rolled onto his stomach, tucked his knees under him, and began to stand.

Parker's nerves were inflamed, his head still aching, his shoulder bleeding. He raised the gun with both hands and squeezed the trigger.

Bam!

He'd shot near the man's feet, the sound and vibration of it driving him back to the ground, hands over his ears. Slowly, he turned to look at Parker.

"You know the drill." Parker backed toward the Jeep and rested against the side door. A siren screeched through the air, rising in the distance.

The vehicle was help, after all.

Parker watched as another sheriff's Jeep bounced over ruts and knobs in the rough road, fishtailing around a corner, churning dust. He turned back to the gunman and watched him.

Moments later, the Jeep skidded to a halt about twenty feet away from Parker and the man on the ground. A woman slid from her seat, shotgun in hand.

"Put it down!" she said to Parker.

He laid the gun gently on the hood of the Jeep. "I'm the one who called you."

The gunman started to stand again and the deputy raised the shotgun to her cheek, staring him down. He lay back in the dust. She hopped forward a step, favoring her left leg.

"Who did you talk to on the radio?" She was testing the truth of his story.

"She said her name was Grace."

"I was already on my way. Dawson's been missing. We knew something could have gone wrong."

"Yeah, some things have definitely gone wrong."

The deputy lowered her gun. "Got a job for you." She tossed a pair of handcuffs to Parker. He missed the catch but lifted them from the dirt and trotted quickly to the hollow-faced man, stopping in front of him. He tried not to look into the man's eyes, but he couldn't help himself. He glanced at those glossy, onyx bulbs and nearly choked. He averted his gaze, but he saw the man's grin, a white tooth catching the light. He clicked one cuff onto his left wrist, but the man kept his right one out of reach, a kind of passive resistance. The deputy stepped closer to the man, shotgun aimed at his groin. He sneered at the deputy and then at Parker and moved his other wrist within reach. Parker locked that one too.

"Squeeze until you hear a solid click and make them tight."

Parker double-checked the cuffs then stepped away. He leaned at the waist and tried to slow his heart.

"Where's Dawson?" she asked.

"That way." he pointed. "South a few miles."

"Is he okay?"

"Wounded in the leg. Bleeding. Dehydrated for sure." Parker stood erect. "If he gets help soon enough, he ought to make it."

"Grace has got a chopper on the way."

The deputy shifted her feet, staring over the horizon. Her hair was short and dark eyes brown as wet earth, skin smooth and tanned. Suddenly, she turned back to him and smiled a gleaming row of perfect teeth and as exhausted and beaten and weak as he was, he had to smile back.

"I'm Rowe. You must be Parker." She nodded at him but kept her shotgun cradled in her arms, pointed in the direction of the hollow-faced man. "What the hell happened here?"

Parker moved back to the Jeep and leaned on the hood again. "This is his gun." He pointed at the Glock and back at the man on the ground. "There are two more of them near the pumps, but they're tied up too."

"Holy shit. Can you call Grace again? Tell her we'll need prisoner transport for three people right away. These Jeeps are too small for the job."

Parker did just that. Deputy Rowe added her voice to the call so that Grace knew it was an order, not a request. Time for some out-of-county back-up.

When they turned off the radio, she asked him again what had happened.

That's when they heard an engine roaring behind a small hill, growling and growing as the black SUV appeared above the sage brush, barreling toward the back-up generator by the pump station, aimed directly at the red tank of fuel that fed the tractor-sized engine.

The suburban rocked over uneven ground then found a level path toward the fuel and shot into the metal legs that kept the tank elevated. The collision fired the cylinder into the air, spinning, crashing into the front windshield of the SUV and the whole mess of it exploded in a blast of fireworks that vibrated the ground and heated the air. The SUV bounced to a stop over the metal braces, smoke billowing in braids of black cloud. A secondary explosion blew the glass from the doors and sides, shattering the air.

Oh, god. Had Relic been inside the SUV?

Parker's throat closed. He and Deputy Rowe stared at the tangled mass of burning metal. So did the hollow-faced man.

"What the hell?" She turned to Parker.

He ignored her question and moved away from the Jeep to get a better view of the wreckage and the station around it. He ran toward the path taken by the SUV, searching the ground, searching for movement, any kind of movement, and then he caught just a glimpse, a large daypack bobbing across the mesa and quickly out of sight.

"Shit, there, Relic," he whispered to himself and cleared his throat.

Relic had just silenced the electric pumps, plugging the greenhouse gas.

CHAPTER 68

"What the hell is going on here?" She nodded toward the rising smoke.

Parker turned and walked back to Deputy Rowe. "Yeah, say, before I tell you all of it, there are two people just over the border in Colorado you need to know about…" Parker explained how Betty and Cindy and probably Charles had worked together in a plan to embezzle fifty-five million dollars meant to improve the pump station, which was pumping CO_2 into the air instead of into the ground. He told her they were probably leaving the United States very soon. He handed Rowe the papers that Dom had taken from Betty's confidential report.

Deputy Rowe seemed stunned for a moment then reached into Dawson's Jeep and radioed Grace again. Time for the FBI.

When she was done with the radio, she stared at

the burning generator and the pump station just beyond them. "Did you see anyone in that SUV?"

"It's empty," Parker said.

"So someone aimed it at the fuel tank and then rolled away from it?"

"Must have." He figured that Relic preferred to remain out of view, to keep wandering these mesas and canyons free and clear. But the crash made it obvious that someone had been helping Parker.

"Where is he? Who is he?"

"He's a recluse, a hermit, I'd say. He saved me from this ass." Parker pointed at the gunman on the ground. "And helped me with the two others by the pump station."

"So where is he now?"

"Gone back to see if Dawson needs any more help. He took what he called an 'oh-shit' bag…"

Rowe gave him a quick smile.

"So, he's gone now? You saw him leave?"

"Yes, ma'am." Why had he just called her that? Was it the uniform?

"My mother is 'ma'am.' I'm just 'Rowe,' okay?"

"Of course."

"Know how to use that?" She pointed to the pistol on the hood of the Jeep.

"Yep." Parker moved closer to the gun.

"Pick it up and aim it at that guy." She pointed to the hollow-faced man. "I have to check on the men you said are over there." She nodded toward the pumps.

Deputy Rowe shouldered her shotgun again, keeping her aim at the ground and limped cautiously toward the pumps. Parker lifted the Glock and held it toward the gunman on the ground.

Rowe told the first man at the pump to mind his manners. She checked his restraints and seemed satisfied. She disappeared for a few minutes, behind the far row of pumps. When she returned, her shotgun rested easily on her shoulder, barrel aimed at the sky.

"Nice work," she said.

Maybe he ought to think about that—getting into her line of work, that is. And maybe she could help. The thought flashed through his brain like a single, bright strobe—a career in law enforcement? He could help chase the Bettys and Cindys and Charleses of the world. And the Mr. Smiths.

It would be physically tough, for sure. Mentally, too.

But his sister would be proud of him.

He smiled. Maybe he could even work with Deputy Rowe...

CHAPTER 69

David Gregor straightened his TSA uniform and scanned the crowd. His stomach tensed as a couple walked closer to the security line, hand in hand. They fit the description he'd been given, but then, so did so many other people. Retired police officer from Houston, now Dallas Airport Security, David had been called just moments ago to check the identifications of departing passengers before they went through the security check point and to detain two particular people traveling together.

The man wore a close-cropped beard and looked to be in his sixties. The attractive woman with him looked a little younger. She leaned into him, nuzzling against his chest. They smiled at each other; a pair of honeymooners more mature than most.

"Photo I.D.'s please," David said as they approached.

They released their hands from each other, the man

searching for his wallet, the woman rummaging through her purse.

The man showed him his driver's license and David checked the photo against the man's face. The woman handed hers to him and he made the same check.

They were the couple he'd been told to hold.

"Will you folks step to the side for just a moment?" David asked.

The couple moved politely a few feet from the line so other passengers could proceed to the security check point.

"Where are you traveling today?" David asked.

"Belize." Betty Coulter smiled.

"Tickets?"

"Is this some new procedure?" Charles Story squinted his eyes, a hint of suspicion in them.

"Not really." David kept his eyes on their driver's licenses.

Betty handed David her airline ticket and Charles followed suit.

David pushed the squawk button twice on his hand-held radio.

"What's this for?" Betty asked, meaning the stop and extra check.

"Folks, we need you to wait here while we check

your tickets." David waved them above his head. Another TSA worker stepped over, took them, then hurried away.

"Hey, you can't take those!" Betty's face reddened. "We'll miss our flight."

"We'll make sure you're okay," David kept his voice low and soothing.

"You can't detain us here," Charles pointed a finger at him, "without a warrant."

"He's a highly respected criminal attorney." Betty's eyes flashed, her words like controlled explosions. "We've got luggage already checked in, and if we miss our flight, our vacation of a lifetime, your name will be front and center in a major lawsuit."

"Sorry, I can't help you with that. I'm just asking you politely to stay here until my supervisor returns with your tickets."

"Bullshit," Charles snorted, his lips tightened. "Your supervisor is never going to return with our tickets, is he?"

David remained stoic.

Charles spun toward Betty. "Damn it!"

"What are you saying?"

"I know how this works. He's got us under arrest, but he's too much of a chickenshit to tell us."

"This is outrageous!" Betty's face flushed.

"On what grounds?" Charles challenged David.

"You're right, sir. You are both under arrest."

"For what? You have a written warrant, signed by a judge? Because I don't see one…" Charles took a step back like he was ready to leave. But without his ticket, he wasn't flying to the Caribbean.

"Arrest?" Betty's eyes narrowed, looked to the ground, then back up at David.

Charles moved a little farther away from them.

"What did you do?" Her question was to Charles.

"Nothing! This is an illegal detention."

"They're arresting us!" Her voice rose above the din. A few people turned to watch. "We're not getting out of this, Charles. Are we?"

David glanced expectantly across the open floor then back to the couple.

"Are we?" she demanded.

Charles was silent.

"What did you do?" She screamed at Charles but gave him no time to answer. "You've screwed this up, you lying piece of shit! Haven't you?"

"Betty…" He raised his palms in the air.

"You cheating, lying…" The veins in her neck rose like hardened ropes, her lips pulled back in a snarl that seemed to turn her head into a brutish skull.

David had never seen such a radical transformation.

"Don't say anything, Betty…"

Fists clenched, she stepped toward him. "You screwed this up somehow, didn't you? You and your cheating harlot…" She raced forward and began pounding her fists against his chest.

Charles tried to step away, one foot behind the other, and tripped into a stanchion that held the fence-like belts, and he spun to the scuffed-up floor in a tangled mess. The noise and commotion stilled the line of passengers, hushing their small talk.

Betty pounced immediately. Charles was too twisted in the belt to defend himself. She hollered something David couldn't understand and beat on the side of Charles's head like a pile driver.

David leapt to Betty and pulled her away, pinning her arms behind her, struggling to keep her under some semblance of control.

Two men in suits jogged toward David to help, their badges held high for the public to see.

CHAPTER 70

Rowe tucked her hair behind her ears and pushed through the stiff hospital door. She'd spent all day yesterday with the FBI and Parker, who now had twenty-two stitches in his shoulder. Dawson had been admitted the day before yesterday, virtually comatose. The doctors said ten more hours on the mesa and he would've been dead. Luckily, he was a stubborn son of a gun. They'd cleared him for short visits just this morning.

Dawson lay still on the bed, eyelids closed, tubes running in and out of his arms, bandages wrapped around his thigh. She tiptoed closer.

"You need to work on your stealth mode, there, Rowe." Dawson opened his eyes.

She smiled. "And you need to work on your officer safety training."

"Huh." He gave her a half-smile.

"How's your foot? Didn't some old horse stomp on

it to get your attention?"

"Ha, ha."

"What brings you down here?"

"Gotta see what condition your condition is in."

"And?"

"Not the best."

"No, I guess not."

"You feeling okay?"

"Every part of me hurts everywhere. Including places I didn't know I had."

"Well, you've been through the mill, as they say."

"Huh."

"I've got some good news for you, though."

"Spill it."

"FBI took Betty Coulter and Charles Story in on an arrest warrant. Story's assistant, Cindy somebody or other, has been singing like a songbird. Seems she and Story were planning to run away together when she was poisoned. At least, the docs suspect she was poisoned."

"Love triangle?"

"That's it. They think Betty Coulter did it, but they might not be able to prove it. But there's more. The DEA has been surveilling a 'Mr. Smith' for a while now. Suspected fentanyl dealer in the four corners area. Well, he's a former client of Charles Story, and Cindy says he's been in regular contact lately with the lawyer. DEA says the gunmen we caught—well, the guys Parker caught—work directly for Smith."

"Whoa."

"Yeah, they're working on those goons now. If just one of them cuts a deal, FBI and DEA will both have Smith breaking stones at the state penitentiary."

"That's damn encouraging."

"And there's one more thing. The feds are also diving into Story's connections with two companies set up to take a fifty-five-million-dollar project out there on Moonshine Mesa."

"The pump station?"

"Bingo. According to records that Parker got from Betty Coulter, they turned the old station into a carbon sequestration project. Problem was, Parker and his co-worker, Dominic Ubaldi, found out that the project was leaking."

"Leaking?"

"CO2. The feds think that's what killed the professor."

"Holy hell."

"We had leads on the professor's old girlfriend, a student falsely accused by Hollins, and the driver of the van that took them to the dig site. None of them panned out."

"But…gas?"

"Yeah. I guess the technology's safe once they get the gas far enough underground. But here, the underground pipe was leaking CO2 into the upper layers of the geology before it got deep enough. It was getting pushed out of fissures in the rock formations. The coroner said the professor died of asphyxiation. The feds think he breathed in the CO2, got dizzy, passed out, and suffocated."

"It's not leaking now? Is it still dangerous?"

"No, it's shut down. EPA will be investigating."

"And Parker is who told you about the CO2 leak?"

"Yeah."

"And you believe the guy?" he wrinkled his nose.

"Why not? He saved your life, you know. Took out three gunmen and called for help before I even got there."

"Huh."

"You don't believe me?"

"He had help before you arrived."

"Yeah, he said as much. Some hermit he claims roams the canyons. He drove an SUV into the back-up generator. He's the one who shut down the pumps. Did a nice job of it, if you ask me."

"You saw him?" Dawson pushed the button that

made his bed rise to a sitting position, excitement in his voice. "Did you get a good look at him?"

She shook her head. "Tinted windows in the vehicle. Plus, he got out before it crashed and took off."

"A moonshiner?"

"Parker can't say either way."

"Hell, that hermit was there with me on the mesa, Rowe. I saw him, too, after all these years of chasing him."

"Yeah, well, you must have been pretty out of it up there. You were severely dehydrated, and you lost a lot of blood."

Dawson stared out the hospital window. "At first, I thought he was some figment of my imagination, but what you just said confirms it. He was there with Parker. He's real, Rowe, and he's still out there. Now I remember putting the guy under arrest. Well…sort of." He shook his head.

She lowered her eyes, staring from under her brow. "Don't get started on your Bigfoot theory again…"

"Rowe…"

"You can't blame some unknown hermit for all the mischief in this country."

"Sure, I can. I've got stories from eyewitnesses with the same description: wiry, black hair, ponytail, goatee…"

"That fits a lot of river rats around here." She

put her hand on her waist. "Rafters and canoers. Canyoneers. Campers."

"Humph." Dawson didn't believe it.

"The rescue guys found cougar hair and scat outside your little campground, you know." She ran a finger over the foot of the bed.

"Yeah, that was no figment…" His eyes grew wide.

They were silent for a while, pondering the braiding of events, the players, the close calls.

Rowe returned her gaze outside the window. "Good thing you lit a fire when you did too. That plateau is huge. The paramedics said they'd never have found you tucked under the rocks the way you were."

"Fire?"

"A little one. Smoky. To help them find you."

"But I didn't light anything after Parker and the hermit left me. I'd burned up everything I had the night before…"

CHAPTER 71

Parker rested his arms on his knees and stared across the flats at the Colorado River, ripples glistening like flashes in a meteor storm. The Cedar Flute ruins rested behind him, reminders of the chase he'd had through the tower, the climb above the huge, rounded rock, the gut-buster stairs carved into the sandstone—hidden from everyone except Relic, who'd known exactly where it was. And who'd saved his life more than once in the last few days.

He pictured the pump station atop the mesa. Relic had managed to completely destroy one new pickup truck and one huge SUV. Plus a back-up generator and fuel tank, treating all of them like interlopers. And he'd stopped the invisible gas from killing anymore bees or crows or cougar cubs. Or humans.

Funny, he thought. Charles and Betty would have gotten away with their massive embezzlement scheme if the pipes leading into the ground hadn't begun leaking

CO2. Their fifty-five-million-dollar lifestyle now shrunk to the size of a prison cell.

Parker rubbed the bandage on his shoulder. The itch was terrible sometimes, but he knew that meant he was finally healing. He'd slipped off his shoes and socks and laid them aside. He dug his toes into the warm dust and watched as the red powder lodged in the cracks of his skin.

The FBI had grilled him over and over, pulling out details he thought he'd forgotten. Then the DEA agents had a go at him. But it was worth it. The people responsible for Dom's death and the ecological disaster on Moonshine Mesa were facing decades in prison. The FBI and DEA didn't share much information with him, but Deputy Rowe did, and she'd said they had a solid case against Mr. Smith, too.

He hoped Smith and all the other drug dealers rotted in prison, then in hell. He'd heard there were over 70,000 accidental deaths last year from fentanyl alone. And the lives of those who survived were wounded and often ruined—addiction run rampant.

He pulled a blade from a tuft of grass, chewed on the end of it, and thought of the dinner he had planned this evening with the lovely Deputy Rowe. He had plenty to talk with her about—recent events, to be sure, but also the path to joining law enforcement. Maybe it was his path, maybe it wasn't, but he was going to find out.

He turned to look at the ruins.

Stone walls rose straight and flat to the top of the overhanging cliffs. Windows like boxy eyes stared across the river, dark and dull. The archeological dig and re-construction had resumed, the students hard at work around the bend, the crime scene tape all wadded up and thrown away.

He wondered how the people here had lived a thousand years ago. He marveled at how much of their lives was still here, carved into the landscape. Fathers, mothers, families tending fields and hunting game up and down the river and atop the mesa. Dogs, domestic turkeys, games, toys, cooking fires, all of it right here in this place. He understood its pull on Relic—they were some of his ancestors, after all. Parker, too, could feel a connection.

Polished cliffs hung above the ruins, toward the top of the mesa. From down here, it didn't seem so far away. But he knew better. Strange how your point of view changes when you're sweating and struggling to the top—how your perspective on things changes them. Or maybe it changes you.

He turned back to the river and sensed a drop of

the sun along the horizon, past its zenith.

Relic had asked Parker if his loneliness wouldn't leave him alone. Good question. Maybe it wouldn't; not entirely. His little sister had moved on to the next life, ahead of him. Dom was gone now, too. But seeing his part in the natural world was a comfort. He was a spirit, after all, having this human experience. He rubbed his bare toes in the fine, red dust again, thinking how his own body was made with the stuff. All of us, all of it, related.

And he wasn't feeling quite as lonely anymore.

AUTHOR'S NOTE AND ACKNOWLEDGEMENTS

Thank you for reading Moonshine Mesa – I really hope you enjoyed it! As an author, I depend heavily on book reviews and referrals. If you think others might enjoy the novel, too, please leave a quick review on Amazon or any other internet site you use for selecting books to read. The moment it takes to leave a quick book rating makes a lasting difference for the author!

Geologic carbon sequestration injects carbon dioxide (CO_2) into geologic formations for long-term storage. It's been used for years at oil field sites, where oil production releases CO_2, and which sometimes can be captured at the site and piped into a nearby formation. Carbon sequestration technologies also include those which take CO_2 from the ambient air and inject it deep into the earth. These and other approaches are designed to reduce greenhouse gases in the atmosphere that our use of fossil fuels spew out every year. Though currently a drop in the proverbial bucket, they are becoming an increasingly important tool for mitigating climate change.

Leakage from geologic reservoirs is a concern, but properly managed storage is likely to retain 99% percent of its sequestered CO_2 for over 1,000 years. Unless, of course, Charles and Betty are involved…

The canyons, cliffs, ruins, and rapids in all the "Relic" novels are real places I have hiked, climbed, explored, canoed, or swam (sometimes unintentionally) but they have been re-arranged into fresh landscapes better suited for the particular story.

I hope Moonshine Mesa sparks some thought about where our next breakthroughs might occur and the intense need for humans to reach solutions for the problems humans create. Our hard work and "big" brains got us into this mess. Now they need to get us out.

Hats off to my lovely and patient wife for all her support while working on this effort. Thanks to her, Dad, Sarah, and Julie for their valued insights and edits. Thanks to my friends, family, and colleagues, whose support helped keep my head above water.

I also want to thank my editor, Jim Dempsey, for his encouragement, careful attention to detail, and insightful suggestions. I thank Daniel Thiede for his beautiful cover art and book design and his much-needed help with the technical aspects of the work. And I thank the talented Nate Baldwin for yet another extraordinary map of the canyons and mesas in this novel.

Thanks to all who understand our kinship with the planet and those who work in the service of their ideals.

BROKEN INN

"Well, butter my buns…"

He shaded his eyes with the palm of his hand.

There were two pickup trucks in Demon's Roost canyon – one in the deep arroyo at the base of sheer cliffs to the south, one on the upper flats that made up most of the corkscrew canyon. There'd been uranium mining here in the 1950s, but what these yahoos were doing now was a mystery.

Relic tightened his ponytail and stared into the twisting gorge.

Yesterday morning, snow capped the hoodoos – white icing on scarlet cupcakes. By this afternoon, the sun-fired rocks had begun radiating heat near 100 degrees, wringing moisture from the human body like a twisted sponge. The cliffs above him seemed to glow, slivers of clay injected into the blood-red sandstone like fat marbled into raw steak. A pair of crows squawked overhead.

An unlikely descendent of disparate clansmen – one Scottish, one Hopi – Relic wandered these plateaus and chasms, a sometimes-trespasser, recluse, and moonshiner. He'd been called a vagabond, a sasquatch of the desert, but these remote places were home.

He left his pack by a rock and trotted down the trail to the bottom of the canyon. He moved quickly around the first bend to a spot close to the truck on the flats. No one seemed to be around. He walked to the pickup, a silver double-cab, its tailgate down. Topographic maps lay flattened across the truck bed, rocks on the corners to hold them in place. An empty five-gallon container for water sat on the end of the tailgate, neon-orange stripes across its side. A gust of wind slid the plastic canister off the edge and Relic picked it up.

The maps were of Demon's Roost and places to the north. Scribbles and circles were penciled over the contour lines, but he couldn't tell what they meant. The second truck, the one in the dry creek bed, sat around a bend in the canyon, out of sight from this position.

Something made him uneasy. Some distant vibration, maybe. The crows had gone silent. Charcoal clouds hung in the east.

Two men rounded the corner, boots rasping over the sand, heads down, mumbling to each other. He watched from behind the silver truck, some fifteen feet above them and thirty yards away. One wore jeans and a white dress shirt, out of place in this remote canyon. The other wore a red shirt with a leather strap across his shoulder.

Relic took a step back and felt it again – this time a deep rumble under his boots – and suddenly he knew what was coming. Though desperately dry, it was water that had shaped these desert lands, sheer bluffs and jagged drainages wrought by the power of rain. A cloudburst 50 miles away could become a flash flood in these narrow canyons, a deadly blast of water exploding with little warning. The men in the arroyo stood directly in its path.

"Hey, hey!" Relic raised the empty water container above his head, waving it in the air, sprinting past the pickup truck and toward the edge of the ravine.

One of the men looked up.

"Get out of there! Out of there!" Relic shouted, pointing up the embankment, urging them to run from the dry creek bed before it was too late.

The other man straightened, suddenly startled, and reached for his side.

"Flash flood! Flash flood!" Relic waved the plastic canister again and stepped to the edge of the ravine.

The dissonance in his toes became a bellow in his head, an angry groan.

One man began to climb from the bottom of the arroyo, boots slipping up the sandy rise. The other lifted his hand from his side, a pistol in his fingers, aiming it toward Relic.

Relic spiraled backward reflexively, stepping suddenly into thin air, dropping down the slope, skidding feet-first through loose sand all the way to the bottom. He stood and looked at the gunman, who'd holstered his pistol and begun climbing the side of the arroyo behind his companion. In a moment, they both stood above the empty drainage, out of danger.

Now the sound of thunder rolled through the canyon, echoes doubling the alarm. Relic ran down the dry bed, frantically searching its steep walls for a place he could ascend. The rumble became the roar of whitewater, ramjet engines at full throttle, all other sound blasted aside by the urgency and enormity of the coming flood.

Relic turned in time to see a two-foot bank of water rise behind him, precursor to the deluge to come.

He held tight to the empty container and ran toward the spot the two men had used to climb from the dry bed, but as he began to scramble up the slope, the coffee-colored water, heavy with silt, reached his feet, sweeping them forward, twisting him down into the roiling river.

He wrapped his arms around the canister, his make-shift life vest, and lifted his feet in front of him. A surge forced him underwater – his eyes closed, mouth shut – then lifted him rapidly toward the top of the arroyo, shoving him forward faster than a man could run. He kicked to keep his feet downstream, buffers against rocks, trees, or cliffs. The newborn river hurtled him around the bend, a choleric infant wailing at the world.

The second pickup truck lay directly in his path.

He wiggled and twisted, paddling his boots as fast as he could, but the truck came swiftly closer, closer, his feet about to smash into the rear window. If he were forced through the glass and into the cab of the truck, the river would pin him there and drown him. But as he approached, he seemed to slow, then slow some more. His boots touched the window. He bent his knees and pushed away, then he realized he hadn't slowed at all. The truck had been lifted from the ground and shoved forward with him. The water carried them both through the flood together.

The deluge raged around another bend in the canyon, rocks clacking violently against each other along the bottom, tumbling into the flow from the sides, debris that could crush him in a second if he got caught between them. The truck separated from him, rolling to its side. A wave suddenly tossed his head and chest above the flow, his feet pulled downward. He flipped forward and under the rapids, no time to take a breath. Despite the buoyancy of the canister, the swirling river forced him downward, somersaulting into the dark. He lost all sense of direction, what was up or down, dizzy in the swirling storm, helpless under the unyielding, raging current. Pressure rose in his lungs to near explosion, his diaphragm tensing, preparing to blow his final breath from his chest, when finally he spun upward, his head breaking through, and he gasped.

He pushed on the container, lifting his head as high as he could, hungrily sucking in air. The sides of the arroyo sped by, bending left, then right, disorienting him. His boots struck something hard, and he realized his legs were dangling below him again – a dangerous position. He pulled himself into a back float, feet downstream, arms clutching the canister. Waves splashed into his eyes and mouth, blinding him for seconds at a time, forcing him to take quick, shallow breaths. The current threatened to spin him again, so he paddled his feet, twisting to keep his face above water.

The waves began to spread farther apart and his sight improved when he squinted. The truck was behind him now, spinning slowly in the current as he passed another bend in the gorge.

The sky seemed to lighten as the canyon walls receded. He felt his elevation lower as the flood spread across more open ground, closer to its destination in the

Colorado River.

He spun to his left and kicked as hard as he could, moving out of the current. In moments, his bottom touched hard ground. He pushed farther away from the receding water until he could sit up. A three-inch flow continued to swirl around him, but he knew he was safe.

He took full, deep breaths, clearing the adrenaline from his system, regaining a sense of balance.

The flow of water slowly turned to mud. The truck had rounded the last corner, then gotten stuck behind a rock and buried nearly a foot deep in the sandy bottom. He dropped the empty container and wiped the water and hair from his eyes.

"This is the worst thing that's happened since the last thing," he told himself with a grin. It was the second time he'd been caught in a flash flood and nearly drowned. The first time, it'd been his own damn fault. Well, hell, he thought, maybe it was his own fault this time, too.

If the swim hadn't been so deadly, part of him, at least, could have admitted to the thrill.

He sat for a moment, staring into the clear sky. Who were those guys and what the hell were they doing in this canyon? And why did one of them draw his pistol when he'd warned them about the flood?

"I guess no good deed goes unpunished," he scolded himself. He stood slowly, shaking out his arms and legs. He removed his shirt, wrung it out, and put it back on. "I'll dry you out later," he spoke to his pants and boots.

It was time to get the hell out of there.

Excerpt from
RAPTOR CANYON

The tent became a dome of light, then began to smolder and burst into flame near the back, near the kitchen stove.

"Hey, we just cleaned the grill back there," Relic said, making Wyatt laugh.

The fire spread slowly, casting a halo of light across the camp. Security guards hollered, workers yelled their curses and questions, and everyone rushed to see what the commotion was all about.

"Is she really crazy enough to do that?" Wyatt asked.

"Yep," Relic nodded.

"Well, shee-it," Wyatt did his best imitation of Faye.

Relic smiled. "Don't let her hear you or she'll knock your block off."

"No doubt."

"Would you see what you can do to slow down that backhoe up ahead of us and anything else with a lock and key? Then work your way north, swing back toward the staircase and we can meet up there."

Wyatt nodded.

"Keep a close look out. They'll be searching as soon as the mess is under control."

"What's your next move?" Wyatt asked.

Relic jerked his thumb toward the portable toilets.

"Really?" Wyatt said.

Relic turned and faded into the dark. Wyatt heard footfalls, someone moving quickly toward him. After a moment, he recognized her shape bobbing along. She tossed something and he heard it clacking into the bed of a pickup. She nearly ran into him.

"Hey." He put his hands out toward her.

"Hey," she said, slowing, but only a bit. "Here." She tossed a stick of dynamite to him, the fuse sparkling lit.

"Shit!"

"Throw it!" she shouted as she ran past. "Now!"

Wyatt stared at the tube in his hand. The fuse sputtered and spat and shortened with every second, time compressed with the tightness of his breath, the glowing fuse moving forward immutably until something like a spinning clutch popped in his chest and muscle movement became possible again. He reached his arm back and threw it as far and as fast as he could, then he spun and ran to the side of another truck and turned back to look.

The pickup Faye had tossed something into rose into the air with a smack that washed away all other sound, then fell back to the ground with a nasty twist as pieces of sheet metal dropped from the sky.

"Holy…"

Wyatt's stick of dynamite exploded somewhere beyond another truck, lighting something on fire, sending a second sonic boom through his skull, making him jump in his tracks. He stared at the blaze as it settled into a steady burn and looked the direction Faye had run.

A third, fourth, and fifth explosion erupted in quick succession in the row of portable toilets and Wyatt knew it was Relic's work. Where was Relic's peaceful resistance now? Lord, he hoped no one was in those toilets. Then, he thought, what a mess of shit, and he giggled and smacked his hands together.

Oh, my god, was it possible to have so much fun? He never expected stopping Lord Winnieship from stealing this canyon to feel so damn good.

He stared at the fire he'd started and tried to think. He wanted to follow Faye but there was no telling what other mayhem she had in mind, and he did not want to walk into an exploding outhouse. He tried to regulate his breathing, with only a little luck. He circled away from the path Faye had taken, giving her a wide berth, moving to the outer edge of the parked vehicles.

Wyatt turned and trotted toward a lone backhoe, maybe sixty yards away. Though the electric lights of the compound were out, the kitchen and dining room blaze cast a sallow glow on the tops of the other tents and equipment. The upper arm of the yellow backhoe was lit like a candle.

His shins scraped across brittle sage and he slowed to a walk. He'd lost his own toothpicks, so that trick would not work with the heavy equipment. After Faye's dynamite, toothpicks seemed pretty pathetic anyway. Maybe there was a set of keys kept in the ignition that he could toss away. Or maybe he could flatten its tires or pull wires from under the dash to disable the beast. He turned to watch the bobbing of flashlights all around the burning mess tent a quarter of a mile away. The voices of men rose and fell in a rhythm that was almost musical, like an offbeat composition.

He stopped at the base of the backhoe and stared up at the top, where the boom and dipper attached. He circled the machine to the open cabin and peered inside.

"Stop and turn around." The voice was deep and familiar.

Wyatt turned and raised his hands. Even in the semi-dark, Lynch's muscled bulk identified him immediately. He held a pistol aimed at Wyatt's chest.

"You!" Lynch said. "You sonofabitch."

Wyatt saw the left hook a milli-second before it struck his jaw, wrenching his head away and toward the ground. He stumbled to the side. A blow to his stomach struck like a rocket and his chest ached, all the veins in his body shut down by a sonic boom. Slivers of light flashed through his eyes, closed tight against the assault. He sensed himself floating to the earth, his muscles turned to liquid. He was out before he hit the dirt.

WINGS OVER GHOST CREEK

He sucked a shallow breath of air, pulled his gaze from the dead arm, and looked back the way he'd come. From this perspective, the arm was well-hidden on the backside of the long pile of dirt, tucked close to the low rock face and well out of view from the hangar and the tents beyond. Last night's heavy storm had flushed loose soil from the canyon slopes and probably from the body, too. He tried not to look back at the fragile hand, but he couldn't help himself. Skin shriveled against the tiny bones, stiff leather holding the assembly of joints together, keeping the fingers pointed in confusing, haphazard directions, their owner not sure which way to go. Red nail polish added a cheap party flare, a celebration completely out of place.

Holy eff. Hold it together, he told himself, get back to camp and pretend he'd never seen it. Tell Thomas. No one else. Someone here could have killed this girl, must have killed her. Why? What had happened here?

He turned his eyes to his feet and shuffled across the ground, moving to the edge of the pile of dirt. He peered around the mound and saw the edge of the hangar and the back of the tents. No one seemed to be around, so he hustled away from the dirt, across the hard-packed surface, and into the hangar. He went to the yellow plane again and leaned on the right strut, his breath still shallow and labored.

Owen looked beyond the hangar to the field outside and the Cessna waiting for them. Where was Thomas?

"Did you get that cold drink?"

Panic charged through his brain, a devil's hot wire crackling from one ear to the other. His head jerked toward the front of the plane and he clamped his hands tightly on the strut. Everett's question was smooth but – was there an undertone in his voice?

Owen managed to force a breath.

"No…" he patted the wing support, glanced at Everett, then spoke to the plane itself, too nervous to look at the man again. Squeezing the strut helped him to focus. "I got sidetracked by this old Aeronca. What year is it, do you know?"

"1946, I'm told."

"Oh."

"Are you a pilot?" Everett moved out of the sunlight and into the shade of the hangar. Owen knew the man could see him better now.

"No, no, I'm not. Tried to take some lessons, but…" He struggled to keep his thoughts on the aircraft, away from what he'd discovered. "Just look at this panel, the instrument panel," he pointed. "Not hardly any instruments here, though. It's all metal, too, like the dashboards on old cars." He kept his eyes on the cockpit, still reluctant to look directly at Everett.

"Yeah, I've looked it over myself." Everett's voice seemed more normal now, more conversational. "The owner has a friend who came out here a couple of days ago. He's restoring the old bird, but I don't know how far he's gotten. The fabric looks like a stiff breeze would pull it off." He ran his hand across the edge of the wing opposite Owen. "You wouldn't catch me flying in this death trap." Everett wandered away from the plane, plucked a long blade of grass from the ground and began to twist it absentmindedly.

"Yeah, the cloth on this one needs completely replaced." Owen tried to sound like an authority on the subject and felt his nerves calm a little as he spoke. He ducked under the wing and walked into the sunlight. "Seen my boss?"

"I think he's about done," Everett pointed toward the tents along Ghost Creek. Thomas and Angela were walking slowly back toward the Cessna. Angela was explaining something, Thomas nodding.

"Well, it was nice meeting you." Everett moved

quickly toward Owen and offered his hand, his smile show-room friendly, his shake cold and curt.

"Yes. Nice meeting you, too." Owen made eye contact briefly and turned back toward the Cessna. "Better get going."

He strode toward the rented Park Service plane, muscle memory moving his legs, thoughts flowing back to that tortured hand, its ragged movement in the breeze. He tried to be nonchalant about getting the hell out of there. Angela and Thomas came closer to the Cessna.

"Got what we need?" Owen asked Thomas.

Thomas looked up. "Yep. Thanks for the tour and good luck to you," he said to Angela. He shook hands with her and Everett and turned back to the plane.

Owen did not wait to be told to climb in. He adjusted his seatbelt, put the headset on, and waited. Thomas did the same.

How was he going to tell Thomas about the dead girl's arm? When should he tell him? Angela and Everett positioned themselves to one side and in front of the Cessna. They could see any conversation between him and Thomas, so he stayed quiet.

Thomas spent a moment examining the air map and checking the instruments. Out of the corner of his eye, Owen saw the man with the red hat, Luke, run up to

Everett and whisper urgently in his ear. Everett glared at the plane, then gave some sort of order to Luke, who ran out of view. Did they know he'd found the girl's body?

"Clear prop!" Thomas pumped the throttle and turned the key, the engine spitting to life. Owen sat back in his seat, eyes straight ahead, and listened to the engine as Thomas adjusted the fuel mixture and checked the magnetos, turning first one off, then the other, then both back on for flight, Owen wishing he would hurry the hell up. Thomas finally pushed the throttle forward and the engine roared, the Cessna shuddered, and they began to roll down the dirt strip, vibrating, bouncing, jarring over small ruts until suddenly, liftoff, and the ride became smooth and even, the engine solid and throaty, clear air ahead of them, and Owen finally took a deep breath.

Thomas made a gentle turn to their left, flying back toward the creek, the dig site, and the old hangar, circling to gain altitude needed to fly over the plateau above the camp. They rose steadily as they went, Owen thinking how to explain what he'd found, hoping he'd done the right thing by waiting until they were in the air, bound for home base.

They leveled out about two miles past the Quonset hut, aiming for the broad Colorado River as they continued to climb beyond the canyon. A ribbon of dust rose to their right, a truck in motion along the road, soon to be well behind them. Ghost Creek faded from view as they neared the level of the plateau. They could see the bronze river beyond as it wound its way southward, on toward the Grand Canyon, on to the Gulf of California. Owen rubbed his hands on his pants and readied himself.

"Thomas," he spoke into the microphone on his headset.

"Yes?"

"I've got something to tell you, something I discovered down there while you were with the archeologist..."

"Yes?" Thomas checked his GPS and adjusted his heading.

Just then, a hollow thump jarred Thomas forward and he pushed the yoke in, then tugged and released it as he slumped back in his seat. Owen grabbed the yoke and his eyes swelled wide and he stared at Thomas' slackened face and began to scream his name, bobbing the plane's nose up, down, up, when another hollow thump jarred them and oil sprayed into the air and onto the right side of the windshield and he heard the motor cough, and cough again, and felt the Cessna lose its power, dropping in the air, descending toward the ground and he screamed again.

DIAMONDS OF DEVIL'S TAIL

"Wicked chickens lay deviled eggs, but this one's rotten, too." Relic took the binoculars from his eyes and stroked his buffalo-beard goatee. Something about the man on the trail below made his skin tingle.

He slid away from the edge, out of the man's line of sight, and looked about. An unlikely descendant from clans of the Hopi and Scottish, Relic wandered the remote reaches of the Green and Colorado Rivers and the high plateaus between them, a weathered hermit at home in the desert outback, roaming ancient trails, brewing his homemade gin at a couple of narrow, spring-fed crags tucked above the floodplains. He tightened his ponytail, errant strands of white flashing through his coal-black hair.

A dried-out branch of cottonwood leaned against the nearest in a row of six Pueblo houses nestled tightly between the floor and ceiling of the cliff, a string of separate rooms, their stone blocks still mortared together in the corners. Inside were mano stones, held in the hand for grinding corn, and metate, wide-bottom slabs used for the same purpose. A child's bow and arrow, chert for making knives and arrowheads, and bowls of corn, squash, and other seeds were set neatly on indoor ledges under a layer of dust; their owners, it seemed, only away for the winter. In the farthest room was a row of large pots painted with white and black bolts of lightning, edges curved and sharp, with handles on their sides, tops still sealed tight, their contents a thousand year-old mystery. Relic meant to keep it that way.

He leaned forward again. The man strode purposefully toward the high cliff with something long, something strangely out of place, glinting in the desert sun. He put the binoculars back to his eyes.

Of all the things to be lugging in this remote country, to be balancing on bony shoulders in the noonday heat, that angular, outrageous shape was an aluminum ladder, designed for the suburban handyman.

"Well, shit on a shingle." Relic tucked the binoculars away, lay flat near the ruins, and waited.

The man struggled awkwardly up the trail, finally dragging the extension ladder to a stop at the base of the sandstone cliff. He wiped the sweat from his forehead and gazed upward at the solid, sloping rock and the extreme measures the Pueblo people had taken to keep their houses and granaries hidden and safe, high in the cliffs and crags, deep in the desert outback. Centuries ago, they carried masonry, mortar, and jars of water up rickety, wooden ladders to build these solid structures; hard, hot work with just one purpose – protection against interlopers. Now the man below had a ladder of his own, and he rested it against the stone and tugged on the rope that extended it upward, the arms squealing in their tracks, each rung clunking into place as it went.

The man shifted an empty duffle bag across his shoulders and began climbing carefully, one step at a time.

The twenty-eight foot ladder shifted suddenly an inch to the side, but it seemed to find a new, more solid base. The man flexed his knees, testing to make sure the aluminum would not slide any farther, and glanced up. The top of the ladder reached just above the lip of the sandstone ledge.

That man must think he'll find a load of artifacts up here, Relic thought, maybe even lower them to the ground by rope from the ruins, then step back down the ladder unencumbered. But the ancient Pueblo had one last line of defense.

Relic rolled away from the ruins and shifted along the ledge until he was directly in front of the top rung of the ladder, waiting. He listened as the man placed one hand on the step above him, then the next, one at a time, rising cautiously higher.

The man reached the cap of the ledge, but when he looked across the level shelf, where the stone walls rested, there, alone in the red dust, sat Relic looking, he knew, like a weathered Pueblo man, a ghost of the ruins, with a black goatee and a ponytail, holding a three foot cotton-wood branch as thick as his arm.

"Shit!" the man's foot slid off one rung and down to the next. "Holy mother…who the hell are you?"

Relic's dark eyes squinted, his lips rose at the corners, and he slid the branch toward the man's ladder.

"What the hell?" the man tightened his grip.

Relic placed the branch on the top rung and began to push.

"No! Shit, no!" He raised his hand for a flash then returned it to the ladder. "You'll kill me!"

Relic slowly pushed the ladder away from the ledge, forcing it to twist outward on one end, then the other, as it lifted from the face of the cliff.

The man dropped both feet to the lower rung and slid his hands quickly down the aluminum sides, dropping his feet, holding for a moment, dropping, holding, dropping as the ladder leaned farther and farther away from the cliff, more and more upright above, ready to catapult him into a pile of rocks, and just as his feet hit the dirt the ladder tipped past its balance, dipped overhead and spun out of his hands and onto the rocky ground with a clang, a bounce, and another clang!

Sign up for book anouncements and special deals at:
AWBALDWIN.COM

Also available from Award Winning Author
A. W. Baldwin:

A.W. BALDWIN

DESERT GUARDIAN

A *RELIC* NOVEL

A moonshining hermit.
A campus bookworm.
A midnight murder.

Ethan's world turns upside-down when he slips off the edge of red-rock cliffs into a world of twisting ravines and coveted artifacts. Saved by a mysterious desert recluse named Relic, Ethan must join a whitewater rafting group and make his way back to civilization. But someone in the gorge is killing to protect their illegal dig for ancient treasures... When Anya, the lead whitewater guide, is attacked, he must divert the killer into the dark canyon night, but his most deadly pursuer is not who he thinks... Ethan struggles to save his new friends, face his own mortality, and unravel the chilling murders. But when they flee the secluded canyon, a lethal hunter is hot on their trail…

Can an unlikely duo and a whitewater crew save themselves and an ancient Aztec battlefield from deadly looters?

Readers' Favorite says:
Desert Guardian is an "engaging action… mystery"

The novel features "tough, credible characters"

Readers' Favorite Five Star Review

Buy now from a bookstore near you or amazon.com

"A CAPTIVATING JOYRIDE...A GEM OF A READ" - DIRK CUSSLER
A.W. BALDWIN
RAPTOR CANYON
GRANDMASTER AWARD FINALIST
A RELIC NOVEL

A moonshining hermit.
A big-city lawyer.
A $35 million con job.

An impromptu murder leads a hermit named Relic to an unlikely set of dinosaur petroglyphs and to swindlers using the unique rock art to turn the canyon into a high-end tourist trap. Attorney Wyatt and his boss travel to the site to approve the next phase of financing, but his boss is not what he seems... When a treacherous security chief tries to kill Relic, Wyatt is caught in the deadly chase. The mismatched pair must tolerate each other while fleeing through white-water rapids, remote gorges, and hidden caverns. Relic devises a plan to save the treasured canyon, but Wyatt must come to terms with the cost to his career if he fights his powerful boss... A college student with secret ties to the site, Faye joins the kitchen crew so she can spy on the enigmatic project. When she hears Relic's desperate plan, she has a decision to make...

Armed with a full box of toothpicks (and a little dynamite), can the unlikely trio monkey-wrench the corrupt land deal and recast the fate of Raptor Canyon?

"A gem of a read…"
– **Dirk Cussler, #1 New York Times best-selling author**

"[You'll be] holding your heart and your breath at the same time…"
– **Peter Greene, award winning author of The Adventures of Jonathan Moore series**

"A hoot of an adventure novel…"
– **Reader's Favorite, Five Star Review.**

Grand Master Adventure Writer's Finalist Award

Screencraft Cinematic Book Contest Semi-finalist

Buy now from a bookstore near you or amazon.com

"A RETURN OF THE MYSTERIOUS HERMIT RELIC... A PAGE-TURNING THRILLER" - DIRK CUSSLER
A.W. BALDWIN
WINGS OVER GHOST CREEK
ADVENTURE WRITERS AWARD WINNING AUTHOR
ADVENTURE WRITERS COMPETITION FINALIST 2020
A RELIC NOVEL

A moonshining hermit.
A reluctant pilot.
A $5million plunder.

Owen discovers a murdered corpse at a college-run archeological dig in the Utah outback but when he and a park service pilot try to reach the sheriff for help, their plane is shot from the sky. Owen must ditch the aircraft in the Colorado River, where he is saved by a gin-brewing recluse named Relic. The offbeat pair flee from the sniper and circle back to warn the students but not everyone there is who they seem... The two must trek through rugged canyon country, unravel a baffling mystery, and foil a remarkable form of thievery. Suzy, a student at the dig, helps spearhead their escape but the unique team of crooks has a surprise for them…

Can they uncover the truth and escape an archeology field class that hides assassins and dealers in black-market treasure?

"A beautifully written thriller."
– Readers' Favorite Five Star Review

"[A] humorous, fun, and well-plotted adventure. Baldwin is a master storyteller…"

– Landon Beach, Bestselling Author of The Sail

"Baldwin delivers another gripping Relic tale with trademark wit and deft expression. This is adventure with philosophy that keeps you nodding your head long after you've put the book down."

– Jacob P. Avila, Cave Diver, Grand Master Adventure Writers Award Winner

Wings offers "…action-packed adventure and nerve-racking suspense, with a touch of romance and humor mixed in." Baldwin has a "gift for capturing the reader's attention at the beginning and keeping them spellbound"

– Onlinebookclub.org review

Grand Master Adventure Writer's Finalist Award
Buy now from a bookstore near you or amazon.com

A.W. BALDWIN

DIAMONDS OF DEVIL'S TAIL

A *RELIC* NOVEL

A moonshining hermit.
An English major.
A $4 million jewel heist.

When diamonds appear in a remote canyon stream, whitewater rafters and artifact thieves set off in a deadly race to the source.

Brayden, an aspiring writer, works in a Chicago insurance firm with his ambitious uncle when they embark on a wilderness whitewater adventure. On a remote hike, they find their colleague, Dylan, dead in the sand, a handful of gems in his fist. When thieves charge in, Brayden flees deeper into the canyon, where he encounters a gin-brewing recluse named Relic. Brayden's uncle is cornered and cuts a deal with the thieves, but they each have a surprise for the other... and the rafters have ideas of their own about getting rich quick... Brayden and Relic must become allies, traverse the harsh desert, and beat the thieves to the hidden gems. Brayden must confront his uncle about suspicious payments at their insurance firm and what he was really doing at the stream where Dylan was killed...

Can they discover the truth, find the lost jewels,

and protect the rafters from grenade-tossing thieves?

"…an adeptly written thriller…the excitement and tension are superb…the entire plot [is] compelling"
– *Readers' Favorite Five Star Review*

"straightforward and thrilling, with humor inter-mixed…Relic is a unique and intriguing character…passionately interested in preserving the ancient archeological sites and conserving the land and water…[We] enthusiastically recommend it to readers who enjoy thrillers, action-packed adventure, and crime novels."
– *Onlinebookclub.org four out of four Star Review*

"Another rollicking Relic ride from A.W. Baldwin…a bunch of double-crossing, dirt dealing, diamond thieves run into Relic's trademark wit and ingenuity. Enjoy!"
– *Jacob P. Avila, Cave Diver, Grand Master Adventure Writers Award Winner*

Buy now from a bookstore near you or amazon.com

"HEART STOPPING EXCITEMENT" - READERS' FAVORITE
A.W. BALDWIN
BROKEN INN
ADVENTURE WRITERS
AWARD WINNING AUTHOR
A RELIC NOVEL

A moonshining hermit.
A budding reporter.
A $25 million misdirection.

The mob, undercover agents, and secret payloads make Broken Inn a dangerous place for a fresh reporter, a newspaper photographer, and a moonshining hermit.

Hailey witnesses a murder at the enigmatic Broken Inn, but when she learns that the hotel manager and her editor are pals, she investigates on her own. When a corrupt guard finds her snooping, she flees into a box canyon, where she is saved by a gin-brewing recluse named Relic. She reports the murder to a deputy, but for some reason, no arrests are made... She enlists help from Ash, the newspaper's photographer, but they must flee for their lives into the back country with Relic and a four-legged stray with a nose for trouble. They discover mysterious metal drums hidden deep in an abandoned uranium mine, but can't tell what's inside. And just when they're most desperate for help, they learn that not everyone is who they seem…

Can they uncover the secrets of Broken Inn, dodge the syndicate, and head off an environmental disaster?

"Danger scorches in another outstanding mystery by A.W. Baldwin"
– New York Times #1 Bestselling author
Dirk Cussler

"Brilliantly executed… heart stopping excitement"
– Readers' Favorite Five Star Review

Grand Master Adventure Writer's Finalist Award

**New York City Big Book Award
– Distinguished Favorite**

Global Book Awards

Independent Press Award – Distinguished Favorite

Books Shelf Award – Second Place

Buy now from a bookstore near you or amazon.com

THE
ANTI
DOTE
A.W. BALDWIN

Can genetically modified seeds provide the antidote for climate change?

A geneticist has developed plants that could stem the tide of climate change, but when grad student Lila finds him murdered, she flees the scene with the seeds. To escape the killer, she hitches a ride with an eccentric duo and a secret payload that could land them all in prison. Chased by ruthless thieves, the three must rely on their wits, uncover the mystery of these potent plants, and deliver the future of the planet to an unknown scientist a thousand miles away…

But the cross-hairs on those million-dollar seeds are on them, too…

"This harrowing techno-thriller is an impressive achievement – timely, and rich with research, intrigue, and a main character you will be rooting for from the beginning all the way to the exhilarating climax. Highly recommended!"
    – #1 Amazon Best-selling author Landon Beach
    (The Wreck, Narrator).

"The chemistry between Harry and Keaton is electrifying." "…there is never a dull moment…The Antidote [is] a gripping novel."

— *Readers' Favorite 5 Star Reviews.*

"Baldwin is one of the preeminent authors in the adventure-thriller genre and he showcases that talent in spades with his latest novel, The Antidote. A unique premise, richly drawn characters, and constantly increasing risk makes this science-gone-wrong, Crichton-esque thriller a slam dunk. Readers will delight in the protagonists deftly navigating a tangle of intrigue and mortal threats, surviving assassins and gunfights to ensure a brilliant discovery—one that could impact the future of the planet—isn't lost to corrupt special interests and greed."

— *Award-winning author Nate Granzow (Get Idiota, Cogar's Revenge).*

Books Shelf Award - Compelling Read

Independent Press Award -- Distinguished Favorite

Buy now from a bookstore near you or amazon.com